T0355035

EMPRESS

FRANÇOIS

iUniverse

EMPRESS

iUniverse books may be ordered through booksellers or by contacting:

iUniverse
1663 Liberty Drive
Bloomington, IN 47403
www.iuniverse.com
844-349-9409

ISBN: 978-1-6632-0444-8 (sc)
ISBN: 978-1-6632-0443-1 (e)

Library of Congress Control Number: 2020914803

Print information available on the last page.

iUniverse rev. date: 09/21/2020

CONTENTS

KOMANSMAN

They say it's a man's world and you have to be a strong woman to make it. I say, how about I make it my world so I can be myself. I learned at an early age that life is not fair, and you must be one step ahead of the rest to get what you want and rightfully deserve. I think of the best and worst outcomes to any situation, then decide if the action is worth the gamble. If it is really worth it—-if you want it so bad that you can taste it, then you go for it and pray for the best result.

I do not regret anything I have done in my life. I am not a gangster or anything, but I have never met a soul that could fool me or stood in my way. I've never set a goal I didn't attain, and I continuously create new goals.

My name is Paris Empress Jones. I'm 5 foot 3 inches tall with mocha brown skin and slanted eyes. The bible didn't lie when it read, I was made in God's image. He took his time on me. My best friend once told me that my skin tone reminded her of the glow of a seal's coat when water ran down it's back. I swear, if a man had told me this, I would have never left his side. My hair is long and straight, parted in the middle.

When I walk into a room, heads turn. People can't help themselves regardless of their gender; they all stare. I date, but I'm like one of the last unicorns. I just haven't met the right guy to expose to him where the sun can't tan. However, my body, style and walk would defy this fact. I wear my clothes fitted, but classy.

I don't go to the gym, but my stomach is flat and firm. I have a tiny waist, D cup breasts, and a backside most women wish they had.

I'm a normal 19-year-old Brooklyn girl, built like a sex

symbol, who goes to college during the week. I have big plans; I study hard and sometimes party harder. I am not alone in my journey. I have a tight-knit family and friends that have become family.

My mom, Amelia, disapproved of the men I have dated in the past. Amelia never met any of them and probably imagined the worst. I refuse to expose her to anyone I've dated until I feel comfortable with them myself. My mom lost two husbands to the street culture. I remind her that I am not her and I do listen when she speaks.

I have no intention of marrying any of the guys I date now. I already know I'll marry a square, who will protect and provide for me. In the meantime, I want to have fun while I am in college. She can't really get too upset as I take after her.

I can handle myself when I go out partying. I don't drink, smoke, or use illicit drugs. I like to dress to impress and love to dance. If it isn't a bottle of water, I don't want it, and, if I put the water bottle down, it stays down. I have trust issues and I set firm boundaries, but I have good reasons.

The crowd I party with understands this. They understand this is a weekend thing. I don't want or need anything from them. We all play a role on the weekends and then go back to our normal lives during the week. I'm the princess that can be a wild child on the weekend. Some of my party friends have really hard lives and they get to be princesses in the club. You have thugs acting like princes and princes acting like thugs. There are hard- working men blowing their checks like they are Rockefeller.

However, we all have an understanding that it's a weekend thing and don't expect anything but a good time. We just have fun. I play clueless and display a blind eye to things. If I acted like I noticed their flaws, everything would change. It would change my outlook on relationships, and they would probably change on me. I like to see their raw human self without filters. I love the roles that they play. It also lets me know how to deal with them.

Anyway, with a name like Paris Empress Jones, I was met to be free-spirited and I deserved the best. I don't settle for anything less than the best. The name "Jones" was the first thing my dad had a chance to give me. All I know is that he died right after I was born. I was never told the exact details of his death, but I had heard bits and pieces about his death and rumors of his life.

My dad's name was Kenneth Jones, and he had a twin brother named Leonard. They migrated to New York City (NYC) from Georgia, looking to fulfill their dreams in the big apple. Instead, they found the drug game. I never could understand how something so serious, wild, and dangerous could be compared to a game.

This was the late '60s and drugs were everywhere. You named it and "Swizzle" (my dad) and "Chisel" (my Uncle Lenny) could supply it. Their supplies were the best quality to addicts. They supplied meth, heroin, LSD, hashish, black mushroom, pills and whatever else you could think of. I am not proud or ashamed of what he did; I feel indifferent.

I can't even imagine that lifestyle. Swizzle did leave a trust for me to receive when I am 21-years old. My mother didn't tell me about the trust until I was 18-years old. Today, I am anti-drugs. I saw how 20 years later my Aunt Nene struggled to become a recovered addict. She is still undergoing therapy and feels like she needs to prove something to the world.

My Aunt Nene was a beautiful, dark-skinned woman. She had natural loose soft curls that she wore down her back. She was 5 foot 8 inches and weighed 155 pounds. Now, she weighs about 115 pounds, soaking wet. Her face is sunken, and her eyes appear harsh. Her eyes are hiding secrets that she will probably never reveal to the family--secrets of her addiction days, the dark days as she calls them.

I love my Aunt Nene, but on a bad day, she looked like the walking dead. Today, she tries to eat right, consume large amounts of water, and take her vitamins. While her healthy eating habits are reversing the effects of long-term use of heroin, crack, and cocaine, it has taken years to see these results.

My cousin, Tracey, is Aunt Nene's only daughter, and was definitely her twin in appearance. She looked exactly the same as Aunt Nene looked in her old pictures. I have Aunt Nene's adventurous spirit, and we have similar personalities and love to live life.

We choose to be happy no matter what we are facing. Aunt Nene glows, she is full of life, loving and adventurous. Since her recovery, she encourages people to be greater than they ever thought they could be. While she is truly amazing, she would have been even greater had she not been addicted to drugs.

Today, she is a valued member of the community. When she isn't working, she does volunteer work at Arthur Hill Correctional Facility in Staten Island. She went back to school and earned a bachelor's degree in psychology.

Tracey has always been conscientious. Her personality is so different from her mother's, she is more reserved and sterner. She is too serious for her age and was never a pushover. She behaves more like a middle-aged man that has lived life and has everything together. She is very stubborn, protective, and can be harsh with her words. Her actions can make people forget she is just a 14-year-old kid. I always grab her and hold her like she is a child. Although she is four inches taller than me, I always remind her that I am her older cousin.

For over a decade, heroin took away Aunt Nene's God-given beauty and sex appeal. Tracey is a constant reminder of Aunt Nene's beauty. Tracey is the spitting image of Aunt Nene's younger self, prior to heroin and crack use. Once Aunt Nene recovered, she tried her best to protect Tracey from drugs and wanted only the best life for her.

Tracey could be very difficult, and no one can fault her. She's an expert at pushing people away. It looked like Tracey was punishing herself because of her mother's drug addiction. She was carrying her mother's cross. I think she thought people might reject her if they knew about her mother's past. Or maybe Tracey rejected others to protect her mother.

It could be that Tracey didn't want to explain anything to anyone. I once told her that she really didn't owe anyone an explanation about herself or her mother. Aunty burned so many bridges in her days due to her addiction.

The family always tried to protect Tracey. Tracey lived with my mom, my sister, my brother, and I for years. We couldn't stop gossiping strangers from the neighborhood from talking. I think people just talked to make themselves feel better. It takes a cruel adult to discuss a mother's bad habits to a child.

I grabbed Tracey because I once caught a glimpse of pain in her eyes. I was captivated by her beauty and distracted by her sad eyes at the same time. No kid should have sad eyes like that. I always hugged and played with her to try to take the pain away. I always reminded her that she was just a kid.

Tracey had seen her mother at her worst, and she grew up quickly. She saw things differently than other people and deep down she was confused. She really was too young to process some of the things she saw. It takes a lot for Tracey to warm up to people, which is not a bad thing.

Aunt Nene was all the anti-drugs education that I needed. My mother felt bad that her sister-in-law had such a hard life. This was her true love's little sister and she felt that she should have taken better care of her. Aunt Nene was just a shy girl from Georgia. We were the only family she had other than her brother Leonard, who is in jail. Aunt Nene volunteers at that jail and my mom visits him often.

Aunt Nene is always telling me stories about how bad she was back in her younger days. She was foxy and sly.

I knew she was telling the truth; I'd seen pictures of her at parties and such. She told me several stories about her partying days and how she felt when she just came to New York. She described the air and the feel of the city. Every city has a smell. She told me good and sad stories. There is one story that stood out, and still haunts me today, as it was the moment everything changed for Aunt Nene.

My Aunt Nene used to dibble and dabble into gateway drugs, like marijuana. She never knowingly did hard core drugs before that day. My Aunt Nene attended a party which she had been invited to by Kyle.

Kyle grew up with her and for a brief period of time, he had been my stepfather. She had gone to the party with her friends, Lila, and Joana. Lila and Joana both passed away that night from a drug overdose. My Aunt Nene was given a joint that had been laced with crack and heroin. She was rushed to the hospital that same night.

However, that near-death experience didn't deter her from using more crack and heroin, as she kept chasing a high. That was the night her life changed for the worse. She told me this story like she was replaying it in her head with a tape recorder.

It was hard for my mom to hear this story. My Aunt Nene had kept it hidden for years. She didn't hide it because it was a secret; she hid it because it didn't matter to her for years. The only thing that mattered were drugs. She didn't even realize what happened to her until years later. The reason why she became an addict wasn't important to her for a long time. The high was.

Aunt Nene is a drug and alcohol counselor. She turned her life around. So many addicts and recovering addicts, as well as their family members, look up to Aunt Nene for inspiration. They appreciate what she is doing. She gives them hope; she is a role model for those fighting addiction, and she is my family's hero.

The first time I visited her at work was amazing. She was a different person than the Aunt Nene I knew at home. She was nice, but stern. It was like watching a television star. She was a natural born leader. Her clients loved her. She inspired them and pushed them to be better. She looked like a model to me that day. Her shape and weight were accepted in mainstream culture. I always told Aunt Nene she was beautiful every time she complained about her weight. Aunt Nene talked about her brothers all the time. She looked up to them.

My dad and uncle were identical twins. They got their nicknames because of their individual personality and attitude. The way they solved things was different, but the end results were always the same. People never saw them argue. They were both smart, feared men, but there were no similarities in their methods of dealing with people.

My mom never talked about my dad's death or criminal past. I heard about it from my Aunt Nene or the streets. It shocked me the first time I heard about my uncle and my dad. I never thought my family had people like my dad. Many people said he was a good person despite his illegal actions.

I wasn't even supposed to mention his name because he was both envied and feared. Many people don't even know he's my dad. It is better that way. Even without Swizzle money, my mom was able to provide a comfortable living for my siblings and me. She is a nurse practitioner. My mom had a set of twins after me.

My sister was named Alexis Princess Jones and my brother was named Leonard Prince Jones. My mom had this thing about royalty, I guess. The twins are seven years younger than me and are inseparable. We all looked alike, including my brother. The only thing he had from his father was his height. It's sad that we had different dads who all met the same fate.

THE MEETING

I was told that my mom met my dad on her way to school in Flatbush. She was studying nursing at Long Island University. It was a total coincidence that they meant as they were from completely different worlds. Their immediate circle of friends was as different as day and night. At first glance they were worlds apart.

The universe has a way of putting things together and evening out situations. It has a way of exposing what is hidden and gives a person what is truly needed at times. My dad was not a gangster–type dude; he was a smooth, swift businessman according to my Aunt Nene.

My parents planned to move away and start fresh. They wanted to find a happy medium between both of their worlds. My dad craved the tradition of the Haitian and Creole cultures. My mom wanted freedom from her sheltered upbringing. They traveled all over the world to find their perfect location on earth to live, raise a family, and grow old together.

My dad was suspected of being a drug lord, but the authorities could never prove it. He was arrested one time, which was through no fault of his own. He kept his mouth shut because of his mentor, who was the only man he ever backed down from. They called him Chinaman. One day my Aunt Nene was going into detail about my dad, but my mom walked in and gave her a look that would have scared the devil himself. Aunt Nene said no more. Swizzle wasn't in love with the street life, just the money the street gave him. He wasn't flashy nor did he want to stand out.

My mom was my dad's motivation to escape the drug game. He was looking for a pathway to a normal life. My mom reminded him of his upbringing and the simple life he once had. They left NYC every chance they got.

My dad gave the appearance of being a "ladies" man, but all he wanted was a family. He stood 6 foot 3 inches and had a golden-brown complexion. His smile could ease any tension. My mom was my dad's kryptonite. She knew things about my dad that no one else knew. I am not talking about illegal activities; I'm talking about his dreams, writing (poetry), and the way he wished the world could be.

They were a good fit, "Ying" and "Yang." My dad made sure he separated my mom from his lifestyle. He was ashamed of it. He knew that he was wrong. He never personally used drugs or glorified what he did. It was a means to an end. My dad also knew of her and his family. There were things she never knew, and he didn't dare expose her to them. He feared disclosing this information would ruin her innocence and question everything she believed in. It also might make Amelia question their accidental meeting that was planned by fate.

He knew deep in his heart that their meeting was destiny. He was honest to her about everything else. He told her what he did and why he did it. He shared what he'd been through and why he needed to change his life. My dad knew of her before he met her. It took weeks after meeting her that he realized this. He knew why he did what he did, why he went through things, and that he had to change his life. Once they fell in love, they created their own world and space.

He met my mom's four sisters and my mom met his family who lived in Georgia. My dad had an aging grandmother that raised him and his siblings. They kept my great grandmother young and happy. She took on the responsibility of raising them when their father died in a factory accident at work. The company blamed his death on his own negligence and barely gave them anything.

Their mother died during childbirth. Neither she nor the child survived. My dad and his siblings endured a series of bad events and loss. My great grandmother, Mary, sheltered them with all the love she could give them. Mary died shortly after hearing about my dad's death and his brother's long prison sentence.

It was too much pain for her to bear. Aunt Nene moved to NYC because there was nothing left for her in Georgia. There was no family. The only thing she left behind was a town full of gossiping people. Aunt Nene outgrew her town and wanted a bite of the big apple.

My mom loved Georgia. She saw the beauty in Georgia that Aunt Nene couldn't see. She loved the humid weather. She liked that the winters were not as bad as in NYC. She loved the slow pace that Aunt Nene was trying to escape. She fell in love with the future that my dad planned for them in a place similar to Georgia. They were both looking forward to a new beginning. She loved Georgia because of my dad. She used to imagine his childhood. She used to imagine relaxing and having a peach tree of her own. Amelia loved the warm air.

Aunt Nene was looking forward to the snow and finding Prince Charming. Aunt Nene moved to New York after my dad's funeral. She felt lost without her brothers. She was the only girl. She was spoiled and had always been protected. She wanted something different like everyone else.

My mom tried to warn Aunt Nene about NYC. Mom told Aunt Nene that NYC was not as glamorous as it appeared. The lifestyle that Aunt Nene was seeking and trying to live was hollow and empty. Many foreigners and people from southern states were victimized by the predators in NYC. They were held captive through drugs, violence, and prostitution.

They never were able to see the beauty of the big apple. They gave up their souls for what glittered but wasn't gold. Mom told Aunt Nene that her brothers didn't party nor live a flashy life. They lived comfortably and travelled. Aunt Nene swore to my mom that she just wanted a new start and wasn't looking for glamour.

My mom only met my Dad's friend, Kyle. Kyle was about an inch taller than my Uncle Lenny. I heard he used to try really hard to be like my dad and uncle, but something about him was never right. He was a college student hanging out with the wrong crowd, just for the thrill of it. Hanging out with the twins wasn't enough for him. He used the twin's name to hang out with the messy unorganized bottom feeders. These people were trying to make a name through unnecessary violence and shameful activities.

Kyle sought out negativity. He was always getting into trouble and calling the twins for help. He was messier and sneakier than what they saw. Dad let him hang out with him, but it was never enough. Kyle wanted to get deep into the drug lifestyle that the twins were trying to escape. Kyle always appeared to be the hip one. He always had to be heard and seen. He always dressed flashy and wore a ton of jewelry, courtesy of the twins.

The twins were nothing like Kyle, but they had history. He was a family friend from Georgia. His family allowed the twins to stay with them until they were settled in NYC. Kyle had already been in NYC for two years. He convinced them to come out to NYC. Kyle didn't make a single friend.

Kyle didn't connect with anyone on a genuine level. He wanted so much to impress everyone, but he came off as arrogant and awkward. The twin's lifestyle didn't allow them to have those needs and they grew up being each other's best friend. They always had to look out for Kyle because of his personality. He was very needy at times and also came across as a pushover and a lonely puppy.

Kyle had a way of inserting himself into people's lives. He had his genuine moments and was very smart. Kyle saw the other side of the twins. My uncle only smiled in the presence of family and close friends. Many people didn't know how to take him. My uncle was brilliant; his IQ was 140. My uncle could have been anything he wanted to be, but he ended up in jail. Kyle and Chisel connected on that level. Chisel was an undercover geek.

Kyle also met all my aunts. He became family on so many levels. He met my mom due to his close relationship with the twins. The twins felt that Kyle could be trusted. They expected the same loyalty that their fathers had for each other. Their fathers had been best friends.

My mom stood about 5 foot 4 inches. Amelia is small in stature, but her presence engulfed any place she went. She is the reason that I knew I was a gorgeous, dark-skinned beauty. We looked alike, except for her golden brown-topaz complexion. My mom is Haitian, and she and her sisters carried themselves like Haitian princesses. They all went to the best Catholic school in Haiti.

My grandmother was a stay-at-home mom. She didn't have to do anything herself. She had separate maids to cook and clean, a chauffeur, a tutor, and a butler.

My grandfather was a businessman who constantly traveled. I was told he was in the shipping business. He had boats to import and export goods throughout the Caribbean and the USA. He would bring the latest electronic devices and latest fashions to Haiti. He cornered the Haitian market. He had businesses in America and Jamaica and provided a good living for his family.

My mom's oldest sister was named Dalia. She was their protector. She had dark skin and exotic, black marble eyes that you could get lost in.

The second oldest sister was Lidia. She had a narrow face, and, in another part of the world, she could be mistaken for Indian. She was quiet but calculating. She was like a predator waiting silently for its prey. Lidia can take care of herself.

The next two sisters were twins, just two years older than my mom. Their names were Sylvia and Tylia and they were the princesses of the bunch. The twins had dark olive complexions, freckles, and copper-colored eyes with wild, tight curly red hair. They were strong willed and tough. Their personalities didn't fit their small frames and delicate, childlike appearances, even as adults.

My mom was the baby of the bunch. She was blessed

to have so many sisters and a strong mom to look up too. My mom and aunts were sheltered but they were not pushovers. They were compared to beautiful wild roses with thorns. They were nice to look at but needed to be handled with care for your own safety. My grandmother, Mesilee, traveled every summer with her children. They were not the ordinary Haitian family. They had old school values.

Amelia's upbringing was one of the reasons my dad fell in love with her. She was raw and natural. She was the real deal to him, and he wanted to protect and love her at all costs. Amelia was Kenny's strength and weakness. He won my mom over with a poem. The poem she read left him exposed. He humbled her with his nakedness. He professed to her his love, fears, and dreams. His truth was the key to her heart. Amelia was so used to people pretending to be someone else to impress her.

Thank God for that poem, because without it I wouldn't have been born. I was born and raised in Brooklyn, New York. I was a '70s baby but an '80s lady. Life was my motive and the world were my playground. My partners in crime were my two best friends, Nicky "Slim" Smith and Kathleen "Kat" Johnson. Together we were fierce.

We were three shades of perfection. We were like night and day but had a few shared core beliefs. Those core beliefs allowed us to create a powerful bond that was never broken. As young adults we thought we were fierce, demanded respect, and stuck by each other for decades. We all lived in the same building in Newkirk. This is where fate put us together.

Slim was three years older than Kat and me. She looked after us and tried to educate us on what was going on. Slim thought she knew it all, in a good way. She was trying to be helpful. We used to ask her about things we were too shy to ask our mothers. She was the wild, carefree one when we first met.

Slim stood about 5 foot 4 inches, was light skinned, and shapely but very slim. The only thing Holly Berry had on Slim was wealth. Slim was very outgoing and always laughing and people loved her. She didn't take anything too seriously. She was the victim of a single mother.

I called us "victims" because we lacked the male role model and a father's love. We followed our mothers' guidance but had to really learn about men through trial and error. A man can look at another man and know he's no good from a mile away.

We tried to be our own teachers and protectors; that is why we were so close. We had adult support but didn't go to them. We usually had each other to go to when bad things happened. We figured out which men were the assholes and who were the gentlemen early on. Then we learned the game that boys and men played. We decided we didn't want to play their games and wanted to be treated like princesses. Once we realized this, it didn't matter who they were. They would either treat us right or go along their way.

Slim was oblivious to her beauty. Slim's mom was on crack and was physically, verbally, and emotionally abusive to Slim. She was an angry, bitter woman with a mean streak, and took it all out on Slim. She would hide it with a fake smile or play with Slim when she thought people were looking. Otherwise, all she had were curse words for Slim, and she was always mean to her. That's how we became friends.

I was home alone one day and heard someone crying. I disobeyed my mom's rule to not go out into the hallway of our building. When I went out, I saw Slim crying at the back of the steps. Our building had two sets of staircases. Slim would always say hi to me when I walked passed her in the hallway with my mom. To a 10-year old, that made us friends.

I asked Slim what was wrong. She told me that her mom had yelled at her and told her to get out. I thought that was strange because she was just a kid like me. The only thing I could think of doing to help was offer her ice cream. Ever since that incident Slim would come to my house. It became a temporary escape from her mom's yelling. I still couldn't go outside and play, but Slim would come to my house and play. Her mom only missed her when she needed her to do something.

Kat and I became friends because of Slim. One day I was sick and home alone. I was bored so I decided to go and knock on Slim's door. She was always home because of her mother, who made her watch her younger siblings instead of going to school. Her mother didn't do laundry very often and she would stay home because of that.

There was always a reason for Slim to stay home from school. Most of the reasons were out of her control. There were no social workers knocking at her door. It was a different time then. Children stayed at home alone, listened to their parents, and no one got into trouble.

I could smell the scent of cigarettes before I even

reached Slim's door. Her mom and her boyfriend of the week happened to be chain smokers. The house was dark and smelt a little musty. The house smelled like it belonged to an elderly couple, but everyone there was young. It was always kept neat despite the smell. I could tell the furniture had been nice once upon a time. I wasn't allowed to go inside of her house, but I knocked on the door anyway.

Even at my age, I knew Slim had too many responsibilities. She was doing things her mom should be doing. She was always babysitting, cleaning, or doing laundry. She had to run errands and sometimes she had to cook. Once she knocked on my door to ask for frozen, uncooked poultry. My mom would give her anything she asked for without any hesitation.

Slim was home and we played in the hallway. Then Slim told me to wait a minute while she went to go and knock on Kat's window. Their windows were so close that they could literally go into each other's room with ease if they wanted to. Kat was also sick that day and stayed home from school. Kat came out to play and we had so much fun.

We took advantage of our sick day. We bonded that day. We played and talked about so many things. It wasn't the day our mothers planned for us, but it was the day we had. We were supposed to stay inside until our mothers come home. Kat and I took turns watching to see if they were coming.

We would have gotten into so much trouble if they caught us playing in the hallway. The next year Kat and I ended up at the same junior high school, Ditmas. It brought us closer together and helped us realize we had so much in common.

Kat had a bronze complexion and was a natural beauty. You could look at her a million times and never once question her beauty. She wasn't one of those girls that had to wear makeup or do anything extra with their hair. She stood 5 foot 5 inches tall.

Kat was born with common sense. I didn't know anyone that could take advantage of Kat. Her mouth was vicious. What made it so vicious was how she used it. She did not get excited or loud when she told you off. She was calm and cold, and her words could burn a hole in your soul. When she was finished talking there was no response, no argument, just acceptance and defeat from the other person.

Kat and I were always together because we attended Ditmas. We also shared the same goal of being successful. We didn't look like the type, but we were straight "A" students. We didn't like losing or failing.

Most people think that individuals form their identities while attending high school, but they are so wrong. It begins so much earlier than that. Their family upbringing and life experiences, even at an early age, help them decide who they want to be.

A person's personality is not set in stone. It can change because of a particular experience. We, as human beings, do not need permission to change. We choose who we really want to be; kind or cruel or happy or sad.

Junior high school is when you get your first real taste of freedom. We were allowed to walk to school by ourselves, buy our own lunches, pick out our own clothes, determine our own hairstyles, and have our first girlfriend or boyfriend.

We form clicks and pick out the crowd we want to hang out with. This was when peers and older kids prey on the innocent, weak, or those who are different. What's worse is that there were no rules for survival and, even if there were, they wouldn't have made sense. The rules were made by other kids.

It was during this timeframe that families lose their kids to the streets, pregnancy, predators or, in worst case scenarios, death. This is the time when parents need to pay attention. This could also be the time where kids form positive alliances.

This is when dreams are created. This is when we find our fantasies and work on making them reality. The kids who want to be astronauts become science majors. The future athlete joins a team, and the future entertainers take up acting.

Most parents didn't see their children for who they were. They don't see their need to belong to a group or find themselves. Some parents still see their kids as babies. There is nothing wrong with that. The key is to see the part they play in the group or the group they decide to join. Parents don't ever think it will be their child being bullied, picked on, or being isolated from the group.

THE CHANGE

Kat and I were excited about junior high school. This was the first time we were going to the same school. This was the first of many things for us. The first time we walked to school by ourselves, I was nervous because I was going to a school where I didn't know anyone except Kat. Kat had gone to grade school with some of the kids that were going to attend Ditmas.

I was nervous because I had a slight Haitian accent. I didn't want anyone to make fun of me. I was always worried when going into a new environment. People either loved me or hated me. There was no in between. I don't understand why.

I never initiated a friendship because I never knew if people liked or hated me. It never worked out for me to be overly nice to people who didn't like me. I figured things would either work out or not. I had a couple of fights in my previous school.

Although I won, I never wanted to go through that again. I preferred to be happy, playing and laughing. Fighting and worrying was always too much for my soul. I also felt that an enemy today will be an enemy tomorrow, or worse, a friend-enemy. A friend-enemy is the worst. They appear to be your friend but always try to harm you. They secretly dislike you. Despite a few incidents of fighting, I was always at the top of my class. I was an "A" student.

Kat knocked on my door so we could walk to school. She knew the way to Ditmas. I must have been nervous because I can still remember everything about that morning. I remember the air smelling busy. It was warm. I could smell the fumes from the cars driving by. We walked past the Newkirk Plaza train station. I rarely walked past the Newkirk Plaza train station because I usually didn't walk up that far. I saw so many people speed walking to catch the morning train. Everyone looked busy, as if they had somewhere important to go. Kat and I strolled our way to school.

Along the way she said hi to a few kids that were also on their way to Ditmas. I didn't know any of them. I just smiled when they said hi. We finally arrived at Ditmas. We noticed a deli right across the street and decided to go in to order breakfast. It was crowded. I felt like I was in high school. I felt independent. Here I was walking to school and eating breakfast ordered from a deli instead of the school cafeteria. I hid my excitement.

We took our food and walked to the six-grade schoolyard. There were teachers outside directing us to our destination. They were able to tell that I was a freshman. There were also crossing guards working alongside the teachers. They wanted to make sure the first day of school ran smoothly.

As we walked in the school yard, I noticed that there were different clicks playing double-dutch. I was not a big fan of double-dutch. I could play a mean game of Chinese jump rope. The boys were just standing next to each other looking goofy. They knew they wanted to play. Kat walked directly to this one group of girls and they immediately hugged her and told her how much they had missed her. They were girls from her old school and the neighborhood. I used to live on the other side of Flatbush. I would have been zoned for a different school,

Jackie Robinson, if I still lived there. Kat introduced me and we just played until playtime was over.

Everyone wore their best outfits. People were trying to form clicks. Everyone was looking for new faces to impress. Some of the old faces came back with more confidence and, of course, everyone thought they were grown. We were wearing labels like Guess, Polo, Nautica, Cross Color, and F.U.B.U. The girls wore door knocker earrings. They were huge gold earrings that literally looked like door knockers.

The boys were more into gold teeth and gold rope chains. They tried to imitate rappers like LL Cool J, Slick Rick, and Big Daddy Cane.

The day went by quick and all the neighborhood kids had to ride the big yellow cheese bus (school bus). I was disappointed that I had to get on the cheese bus at first, but I appreciated it during the winter months. The big yellow cheese bus was supposed to be a safe mode of transportation. The problem was surviving the ride. The bus driver did nothing to ensure the safety of the quieter children from the wilder ones.

I hadn't gone to school with them, but Kat had. I just observed everyone and was ready to defend myself, both verbally and physically. The girls in the cheese bus quickly became friends and formed a click. They welcomed me. I don't know if it was because I dressed nice or because I was with Kat. The kids that didn't fit in would either sit up front or just walk to school.

The kids from our neighborhood would arrive 45 minutes early to school every day. Each morning we would walk to the deli across the street from our school and order breakfast. We would be there before the morning rush. Then we had a chance to socialize, play jump rope, or finish homework assignments.

There was this one girl named Lisa who would ask everyone for a nickel, dime, or quarter so she could complete her order. Now mind you, she was not poor to us. Lisa had the latest sneakers, gold earrings, and jackets. Sometimes she would be the first to get what was out. We were big on being the first to get the hottest new styles. Everyone was upset about her asking, but no one knew how to say no. They talked about her when she left. Everyone tried to avoid her before they bought their breakfast. Lisa was nice, but we all wanted our money. It wasn't personal.

One morning, Lisa asked Kat for a quarter. Everyone talked about Lisa, but no one knew how to say no to her. We had plans for our money. Kat must have had a bad morning because she told Lisa to stop begging for money. She continued to say that, "While you are spending everyone else's money, you are saving your own and buying everything you need."

Everyone turned around and there was total silence. Everyone was in shock. Lisa started to cry. The other girls quickly formed a circle around Lisa, then turned around and asked Kat why she said that. Kat started to feel guilty and was fighting back her tears.

I didn't really like those girls anyway, so I said, "Everyone says the same stuff behind her back. Do not act like this is news!" They all turned around with the look of horror and shock because they were exposed. I was quiet, but little did they know I wasn't one to mess with.

Kat and I just looked at each other, then we walked away to let them deal with their hypocrisy. We laughed about it and realized that it set us apart from the others. Kat could have said it with more tact, but we were only 11-years old. The other girls were angry for a few days and then they started following us around in the schoolyard.

Who would have thought that one moment would map out Kat and my attitudes for the rest of our lives? I mean, that made me change how I dealt with men, women, social affairs, and the work environment. The fact that we were not part of the group made it comfortable for other kids to walk with or befriend us. They were not too eager to judge or cross us.

I truly felt like we made more friends that way. I was able to hang out with people from different cliques or neighborhoods without judgment. I felt free. I didn't belong to any clique. I was myself. I was able to chill with my dorky friends from my classes or my hood fabulous friends. I could clown around with my feminine friend, Jerry, and talk about fashion, or play handball with my Puerto Rican friends. It was different, but it was fun. I wasn't limited to the double-dutch corner--it was awesome.

There were a couple of girls who tried to cross us, but they usually regretted it. I was quiet and dressed like a lady causing some girls to perceive me as being weak. They did not understand that I was peaceful and happy, and I would do anything to keep it up. I did get into a couple of fights, of which I wasn't proud. I never started the fights. I felt my choices were to either allow someone to bully me or stand my ground.

I never could figure out why some females choose to start with me. I didn't gossip or invade their circles. I truly never noticed them most of the time; I didn't even know they existed. I didn't understand and choose not to understand their behaviors. They could never be my friends.

I fought two girls from the same group. This clique's hobby was to start trouble. They were part of this fake girl gang. They were supposed to be the bad girls of Ditmas and were part of a group called MCC. They bullied girls and boys. They would drink, smoke weed, rob their classmates, and have sex with older boys from high school. They tried to recruit me, and I just laughed at them. Who wanted to go around fighting all day? They had the wrong candidate. I couldn't see myself doing what they did. I wasn't brought up that way. I avoided fights every chance I got. Their alliance didn't make sense to me.

I realized that many times if you approach a person while they are alone, you can avoid fights. I learned that no matter how tough a person appears to be in a crowd, their whole demeanor changes once you catch them alone and confront them. I guess it was the guerilla tactics that I and Kat used.

We were tired of girls wanting to fight us because they assumed, we were conceited or the new boy in school liked us. We decided to come up with a plan. Whenever a group of girls started with one of us, the other would pull you away from the crowd. We were aware of our size. Our height and weight were not in our favor as we were built small. On the way home, we would start laughing and think about meeting the girls again.

One of the best examples was Janelle. Janelle was in love with this boy named Keith. I didn't know this at first. Keith was my boyfriend. Janelle belonged to a group of girls who also found him to be cute. Their alliance didn't make any sense to me since you can't split a boy. Janelle was trying to run things at Ditmas. She assumed all of Ditmas' students were pushovers. I didn't care if she wanted to run things.

I knew those girls were using her. They talked about each other and fought with each other all the time. They all lived in the same neighborhood but there was no sense of loyalty. All I knew about Janelle was that she had transferred from Jackie Robinson Junior High School. She bragged about it all the time.

It was lunch time, and Janelle stood by my Chinese jump rope and started talking loudly so I could hear her. The other girls surrounded her as she performed for them. I guess she was their champion. She was also new to the school and was the dummy being pushed forward by the other girls.

Kat and I had smirks on our faces when the gym teacher approached the crowd. He immediately approached me because he knew that my tolerance level was very low. That should have given Janelle a hint. I didn't tell him anything because I didn't know the girl and, besides, I had plans for her. She was just another girl trying to make a name for herself. I knew that by what she was doing, she was trying to change the dynamics of power in Ditmas. I didn't care if she wanted to run things. I felt bad because I knew those girls were just using her.

Janelle probably had no idea that they talked about

and fought each other all the time. They all lived in the same neighborhood except for Janelle. She started off bad at Ditmas and chose the wrong person to pick a battle with. They really didn't know her very well. I later found out that she was chased out of her old junior high school for starting trouble. I guess some people never learn their lesson.

I didn't care if she wanted to run things because I never thought I ran things. Janelle's mistake was that she was trying to bring me down in her quest for power. Paris Empress Jones was no one's victim. Kat and I met to discuss what to do about Janelle.

I could have easily beaten her, but that wasn't enough. I wanted to scare and humble her. I also didn't want to get suspended. I knew I would get into trouble. I could never just hit anyone first; I would have to be attacked. My mom always taught me to defend myself and be smart about it. I like school. I was an "A" student. It was also where I socialized since I didn't really go outside much.

Kat and I decided to leave school early and meet up with Janelle while she was going home. I wanted to beat her up mentally without touching her physically. I knew she thought I was hiding from her.

This was the first time that I ever cut school. I figured, cutting two classes was a lesser evil than getting suspended. I knew this situation wouldn't go away by itself. Janelle would continue to run her mouth and I would end up going in it. The beauty is that if I appeared scared, she got comfortable and cocky. She had been running her mouth all day. People kept coming to us and asking us about Janelle. We responded with "Who is that?"

THE
CONFRONTATION

Kat and I left school early. I remember that day as if it were happening today. I am horrible at being sneaky. I was more afraid of cutting school than getting suspended. I am afraid of anything that would make my mother upset. I guess I was afraid of getting into trouble with Amelia. I wanted to change my mind so bad, but Kat was going to meet me outside of school. We had different classes so there was no way I could meet up with her to change plans.

We were discrete about leaving; we didn't want anyone in our business and we certainly didn't want to get caught. It was hard because there were always people around us. Our classes were in different sections of the school, so we walked with different groups. We only shared our secrets with each other. Everyone knew we were best friends.

After escaping Ditmas for the day, my paranoia kicked in. We didn't look or act like adults. We barely looked like teenagers. Our clothes did not help our situation. I pointed out to Kat that we had to be very careful. I created this situation and had the nerve to share my anxiety with Kat.

I realized that I hadn't thought things through. I didn't have enough time. It's too late now. I just kept staring at our clothes.

Kat was wearing a fitted jean jumper, pink sweater, and a Giant starter jacket. She wore her hair in a side ponytail. My best friend always looked amazing. I had on loose baggy jeans, a red sweater and a down colorful Aztec jacket. We walked all the way to the train by Newkirk. We didn't go down Cortelyou Road because there was too much traffic, too many people, and the school police officer. We walked down Newkirk avenue instead.

The streets were empty, although there were a few people walking around. There was no traffic or constant beeping from cars. I walked this way all the time but now it felt like a foreign land. I usually embraced quietness, but I was scared. I was scared that the quietness would single me out and I'd get caught for cutting school.

We stopped by the pizza store on Newkirk Avenue to get the "after school special" to kill time. Then we walked to East 17th Street and Foster Avenue. I knew most of the kids did not live that far from school and Janelle would be walking home alone. At exactly 3:18 p.m., I spotted Janelle walking down from Foster Avenue. You really couldn't miss her.

Janelle was 5 foot 7 inches tall, slim, and had brown skin. She was taller than most of us in the 7th grade. She wore a black, triple fat, goose jacket, and kept her hair in short jerry curls. The back was always neatly shaved. She was not a slob and she was pretty too. I guess she was used to getting her way at Jackie Robinson until some girls ran her off.

The minute Janelle saw Kat and I she crossed the street, as if she had not talked hostile in school and didn't notice us. That was a smart move--I probably would have done the same thing myself. We continued to walk on our side of the street until she turned on East 18th Street. Then we crossed the street. Janelle started to walk faster with those long legs of hers, so I called out her name. She acted like she didn't hear me, so Kat and I started screaming out her name. She stopped and turned around and we walked up to her.

I introduced myself first and then I introduced Kat. I

then said, "I know you already know this since I am the main subject of your Ditmas educational career." I then asked her, "Do I know you?" I paused and looked at her with a blank stare, waiting for an answer.

Janelle started to say "No," but I cut her off and asked "Well, what was that show in the yard for me? You were obviously near me and looking at me, but you never mentioned my name. So, now, I want to know if that show was for me." By then my eyebrows were up, my eyes were full of rage, and my nose was flared. I was changing from that shy-looking girl that someone like Janelle thought she could pick on, into the terror that comes out when I'm taken out of my comfort zone.

I was becoming the terror that gym teachers, deans, and other girls got to know when they put their hands on me. I don't recognize myself, I can't control myself, when I'm that angry so I control my environment.

I then looked at her with a cold stare and said to her with a calm tone, "Say what you were saying before, but this time use my name--"Empress." She stood there quietly while tears ran down her face. It was so comical; I had to control myself to look serious.

Kat and Janelle started talking. She was playing the good guy this time; she was always the smooth one. She said, "Look Janelle, obviously you don't want any problems, so let my friend cool off and you might as well go home. I understand you are new to the school and you just want to fit in, so you try to pick on someone. This time, you picked the wrong someone, but life is full of little mistakes."

Janelle started crying and she mumbled something

about Keith. I was thinking "not my Keith," but my poker face said something different. I know I had only been with Keith for three months, but I loved him. Kat asked her what she said about Keith.

Janelle avoided eye contact with me, which was a good thing because I was in "attack" mode. She said she met Keith prior to coming to Ditmas. They lived in the same neighborhood; hung out together, and they had even had sex. She was cool with being his special friend even though she knew he had a girlfriend.

When she transferred to Ditmas, she realized that Keith was distancing himself from her. Then she found out I was his girlfriend. I was angry hearing this. We were total opposites, although we were both pretty in different ways. I walked towards her and she stepped back. I told her that I wasn't going to fight her, but that the next time she saw Keith, tell him I said he was "cut." If Janelle ever approached me like she did before I would fight her. It took everything I had to control myself.

Kat and I walked away. Janelle didn't know it, but she defeated me that day. I was hurt because she had given Keith something I wouldn't; I wasn't about to have sex with Keith.

I was too young. But, at the same time, I felt sorry for her. Even though she was pretty, she acted ugly to me; Keith made her ugly! He used her as a tool. He used me as a prize. What we had wasn't real.

Hot tears of anger, pain and betrayal ran down my face. Kat, too, was angry because that was the story of our junior high school life. We had a curfew, so we weren't out all hours of the night and we didn't do what the other girls did.

I asked Kat what to do. She said not to speak to Keith when I was angry. She was right! I went home, finished my homework, and went straight to sleep. The next morning Princess told me that Keith had called me about three times last night. I felt good.

Later that morning, as Kat and I were walking to school, two boys that we went to school with ran up to us. Being nosey, they asked what happened to us yesterday. I said, "Nothing." Kat asked, "Was something supposed to happen?" They kept trying to get us to talk about Janelle; I was just waiting to see how she was going to act in school.

Janelle came to school and pretty much stayed by herself. We crossed paths once and she said "Hi," but barely glanced at me. By the time second period arrived, Keith came up to me. Janelle must have given him my message. I was so happy inside. I wanted him to hurt like I did. Luckily, Kat was walking with me.

Keith wanted to talk to me in private, but I told him "No. Nothing is private anymore; what we had was a lie. You knew all along why Janelle wanted to attack me, and I knew nothing of her. You put me in harm's way." Keith was rambling on about missing me, loving me, and making a mistake.

I was in a daze, so I just told him to leave me alone. He tried to hug me, but I quickly moved out of his reach and then walked away. Even though it appeared Keith was hurting, it didn't make me feel any better--I just felt more confused and upset.

The rest of the school day was peaceful. Oh, I knew

people were talking, but they kept their distance and left me alone. After school, Kat and I walked home.

We barely made conversation, and then we realized Keith was following us. He had his sidekick, Lee, with him. I never liked Lee; he was just so animated and fake. He always felt like he had to be seen. I called him a sidekick because a friend is honest and on equal plains, but a sidekick feels he has to impress and tell people what they need to hear.

To me, that is a dangerous person to have near you. They can, in the long run, make or break you. A sidekick knows you better than most people. In reality they are a narcissistic person's rock and allows them to live in their fantasy world because they enjoy the benefit of it. They have to keep the dream and vision going.

Kat and I walked into a store on the corner of 15th Street and Newkirk Avenue. We took our time in the store. When we walked out, Keith was waiting outside. He looked so cute with his team jacket on. Keith was 6-foot 1 inch, slim, and bow legged. He had curly, soft, wavy hair that he allowed to grow wild. He was with his sidekick Lee, who is just as tall. They called them the twin towers. Lee was Dominican. He wore a high top like "Kid" from Kid and Play.

Lee was always loud, and everything was a game to him. The problem was, he included people in his game whether you wanted to play or not. He used his size to intimidate people. Lee had two weak spots.

Lee was in love with Kat. Kat thought he was too annoying and never gave him a chance. Kat described him as a delicious looking apple you wanted to bite, but then a worm appears. His other weakness was that he hated being called Haitian. He could pass for being in high school.

I was staring at Keith's brown skin with sandy brown hair. He had full lips and lashes that most women would kill for. I looked at Kat and she knew I was going to cave in. This was my first, real emotional drama and what did I know? Kat and I walked out, and Keith walked right to us.

Keith had this funny look in his eyes. Right away, Keith began talking loud to me. He said he didn't know why I was acting like this and that I needed to grow up. He said I was acting like a little girl and I needed to get with the program. His sidekick, Lee, was laughing.

I was embarrassed, confused, hurt and angry. I blurted out the first thing that came into my head. I yelled out, "Keith, your cut," and I walked away. That did not make him go away. That made Keith angrier and more determined. He was fueled with anger instead of love. I think I embarrassed Keith.

Keith and Lee continued to follow us home. For the first time in my life I was afraid of someone my own age. I was also confused! Keith said he loved me, and I still loved him. I was going to give him another chance. Why was he acting like this towards me? I didn't do anything to him. Was he trying to impress or bully me? I started to think about Janelle and wondered if he treated her like that on the regular. Is that why Janelle took her chances by confronting me instead of him? If he did treat her like this, why would she want him anyway?

I didn't want to know that side of him. In fact, I didn't think I liked him anymore. Kat knew I was scared;

normally I would have put my hair in a ponytail and attacked Keith. But I had never fought a boyfriend before. I didn't think you're supposed to fight boyfriends. This was all new to me. I was losing control. I almost forgot that Keith, Lee, and a small crowd were walking behind us.

When we got to Ocean Avenue, the crowd left. They knew better than to follow Kat and me to our block. The minute my foot touched 21st and Newkirk, I turned around to Keith and asked, "What do you want?" in a loud voice and tone. I stepped up to him and performed.

A crowd of older guys quickly came over and wanted to know what was going on. Keith's whole demeanor changed. He kept saying, "Nothing. I was just trying to walk her home." He was looking at me for help. I still had a soft spot for him, so I told him just leave, and Kat and I went into the building. We were laughing! I told Kat, "You know I didn't want to fight him." She answered, "Who would? He's a giant." I told Kat I was getting too old for this. After laughing, I went into my apartment and Kat went into hers.

The guys that came out were the local drug dealers. They didn't want strangers threatening anyone on their block. They really didn't want any negative attention on the block at all. It benefited them to keep the peace so they could continue to run their drug business. They had a reputation.

Everyone knew what they were up to, but people seemed to not bother them. They were extremely polite to the working-class people and hid their transactions. I just remember being happy that they made Keith leave me alone.

My mom wasn't home. My laughter quickly turned into tears, and I must have cried for 20 minutes. I barely pulled myself together, but I knew I had to get dinner warmed up for Prince and Princess. They were my younger siblings (the twins). At 3:20 p.m., on the dot, Princess knocked on the door.

As soon as I opened the door, she quickly gave me a kiss on the cheek, dropped her school bag, and ran to the bathroom. This was her daily routine. Prince walked in, kissed me on the cheek, and headed straight to the refrigerator. As soon as Princess came out of the bathroom, she asked for something to eat. I fixed us all a plate of food.

We were having oxtail, red beans and rice. All three of us had healthy appetites. While devouring the food, we heard a knock on the door. It was Kat and Slim.

Slim quickly started speaking with excitement. She said she heard what happened to me. I almost went into detail, but Prince asked about what happened and Princess followed by asking if I needed her to help me. Princess was a little smarter than Prince. She just stared at everyone quietly and waited for us to start speaking.

I winked my eyes at Kat and Slim and started speaking to the twins. Princess blurted out, "I saw that." I offered Kat and Slim some food and we talked about the latest Newkirk gossip as we ate.

When we all finished eating, I told the twins to go get started on their homework. Prince and Princess were making excuses not to leave. They were worried about me. I gave them both kisses on their cheeks and playfully pushed them out of the kitchen. I didn't think it was fair to expose them to my drama.

Once the twins left, I quickly started to unload my burden on Slim. Every time I started to tell the story; Kat would finish my sentence. I appreciated it because I was hearing what happened from someone else's point of view. Slim was excited. I think she felt like I was becoming a woman or something. She was laughing and occasionally hugging me, holding my cheeks while I told her the story. After a while, we all started laughing.

Slim asked me if we had ever discussed cheating. I said no and I never had a reason too.

My mom walked into the kitchen and we immediately stopped talking about my drama. Amelia quickly said, "Don't stop now." She had a look on her face that indicated she had already overheard a part of our conversation.

Amelia asked us what we were talking about and, of course, we said "Nothing." Slim and Kat tried to make a quick exit because they knew my mom was not going to stop with one question. But Amelia asked them to have a seat and said, "Let's continue the conversation. I heard bits and pieces of what you were talking about, and I am a bit disturbed. I am not upset about what happened because shit happens, but I am disturbed about your reaction to what happened.

Bad things happen to everyone. As a young girl you need to set boundaries. People are people and can be unpredictable when they are hurt or angry. They have different layers because of what they have been through. Hidden layers that only come out when they are emotional."

Amelia compared people to an orange. "Sometimes you see an orange and it looks shiny and beautiful, but the inside is sour and rotten. Sometimes it is beautiful and sweet. Other times, the orange looks dry and small, but when you peel it, its juicy and sweet. The thing is, you have to take your time to peel it. That is the same with people.

Some people look so beautiful, but they're damaged inside. When they are damaged, they hurt others. Some people have gone through a lot in life, but still stay kind and beautiful inside, like your Aunt Nene. Your job, my dear, is to recognize people so you can protect yourself. As your mother, I want you to be beautiful inside and outside. I pray that nothing happens to you or changes you. I know that this is the age girls get into boys and boys get into girls.

This is the age that most kids get curious and their emotions run wild. I wouldn't be a good mother if I didn't have this talk. First of all, Paris, and Kat, you are too young to be dating. Paris, you are not allowed to date, you are only allowed to go to school dances. Slim, you are in high school and you are old enough to start dating, but your mom should monitor you. Empress, you can go to school dances and that is it."

"I just want to know; do you think that how that young man treated my daughter was cute? Do you think it was love? Well, let me tell you, that is not love and what happened out there was not cute. People will only treat you as bad as you let them. Once you have a reputation of being a pushover, it will stick to you. Men, and people in general, will try to get away with what you allow them too. You have to understand this is your life, and you have to set the tone.

The world is tough and will try to use every inch of you if you allow it. I am looking at three beautiful, smart, young ladies. But, guess what? It doesn't mean anything if you don't know how to use it. Other people will profit and gain from your blessings. The key is to make sure you know what you want, what you need, and what you deserve. If you don't stand for anything, you will be lost and confused. One of the saddest things is for someone to realize they were chasing other people's dreams and ideas too late.

The most hurtful part of wasting your life away is not having anything genuine of your own. If you don't learn now how to value yourself and life, your beauty can be more of a liability than an asset. There are some people that are always ready to use, abuse, and then destroy what they do not have, but see in others.

This talk is not just about boys; it is about life in general. You must decide what you are willing to take from people and how you want to be treated. You don't have to be vocal about your needs. It is best to listen, observe, and then notice if a person's behavior matches their actions. People show you who they are every day; it is up to you to see, and then accept it. Last, but not least, never get yourself into something you can't get yourself out of. Think about what I said. I'm going to rest my bones."

I didn't want Kat and Slim to leave. My mother is Haitian, and I am not too old for a good Haitian beating. That little woman is like a ninja. I didn't know where she got her strength and speed. Amelia asked me to wait in the room. I suddenly wished I had on thicker clothes.

Amelia came in with an album instead. I never saw this album before. The album was red and gold. It was full of pictures of my mom and dad. It had pictures of all the places they went, special occasions, and silly moments. I never envisioned my mom as being young before today.

Amelia looked like a teenager in those pictures. She was beautiful. There were pictures of them in Morocco, Coney Island, on the Staten Island Ferry, in Canada, Haiti, Dubai, Italy, Paris, Hawaii and various states in the United States. They were smiling in every picture. Some of the pictures were taken at family functions. Their life together looked like a fairy tale. They were young, beautiful, and in love.

I want something that beautiful that lasts a lifetime. I see why my dad fell for my mom and was ready to change his life for her. I saw pictures of the twins and Aunt Nene. There were also more recent pictures of my uncle in jail. I didn't know my mom visited him. We must have spent two hours looking at the pictures while I asked questions.

Amelia was always saying she was old, but she didn't look old at all. Truth be told, Slim's mother looked older than my mom and she was four years younger. I was just glad I got off easy. I didn't get into trouble.

The next few weeks were peaceful in Ditmas. I was still a little sad, but I didn't show it or talk about it. My mom made an excuse to take me clothes shopping, so I looked flawless. I really didn't care because I was getting ready for graduation and other important stuff. Things were changing and I didn't know how to handle it all, so I controlled the things that I could.

Slim left us. She finally got tired of her mother and moved to Queens with her Aunt Greta. I was devastated; it felt like everyone I was close to was leaving. Slim was crying too, but I didn't discourage her from leaving. Her home situation was horrible. Slim's mom, Nelly, had brought home a new boyfriend.

Nelly usually brought home only two types of men; either old drunks that she could control, or drug dealers in their early 20's to 30's who were trying to get on their feet and needed a place to stay. I thought they were using her. I don't like to judge people because my mom raised me better than that, but I would go crazy if I were Slim.

Surprisingly, this man appeared different. He was not a drug dealer or a broke, want-to-be sugar daddy. He had a real job, a 9:00 a.m. to 5:00 p.m., and that made Nelly attempt to beautify herself. Nelly wore more age-appropriate clothing instead of dressing like a teenage run-away prostitute. She no longer hung out on the street corner all hours of the night with the drug dealers.

Nelly appeared more involved with her children. She was cooking for Slim and her siblings. Although her hard live made Nelly appear to be in the mid-30s, she was only in her late 20s. She never really did her hair or dress real fancy, but she was cool to stand in front of the building with. She was funny and she was Slim's mom, and everyone respected her in front of us. I think it was because Slim was so well liked.

Slim was like the block kid. People looked out for her. People looked out for Kat and me too, but it was different for us. Everyone treated her like a niece or an adopted daughter. We were always respectful and semi-sneaky.

Nelly's new boyfriend was named Rob. They were an awkward pair. Nelly also changed. Rob looked like an ordinary hard- working white collar worker. He appeared quiet and respectable, but there were days when I heard him yelling through the walls. I heard things moving and Nelly screaming. I saw Nelly with a black eye checking the mail once.

One time I heard a bang, then I saw Rob leaving. His face was beat red. He tried to play cool when he saw me. He gave me a fake smile and I acted like I believed him and returned the smile. Nelly was not a violent person. She had her habits, but she never spoke ill about anyone. Nelly even stayed out of my mom's way when she was mad at me. She would go into her apartment and then tease me later about getting into trouble.

I was glad that Slim was no longer living there. I realized Rob came and hid at Nelly's house. He was one of those rotten oranges my mom spoke about. I didn't want to judge him, but I could see he was trouble from a mile away. I knew I was right about him--he was not a good person.

Amelia overheard them fighting once and told the twins they were not allowed to play in the building hallway anymore. Rob kept trying to be nice, but we all knew he was a creep. Amelia and I were walking in the building once and he held the door open for us, flashing his fake, charming smile. We said thank you but kept our opinions of him to ourselves. He tried to have a conversation with

Amelia, but she kept walking and we both acted like we didn't hear him.

Amelia called the twins over as soon as we walked in the apartment. We were all sitting in the kitchen before Amelia reminded us not to go into anyone's apartment. She reminded us that no adults can be your friends. Children and adults cannot be friends.

Amelia told us that she didn't want us anywhere near Rob. "I raised you to be polite, so if anyone asks you to do anything, smile and tell them you have to ask your mom. Smile, then keep it moving. If someone asks you for help with anything, tell them you have to help me and come home immediately." The twins looked bummed out because they had friends in the building.

Amelia noticed their disappointment and said they could go to Kat's apartment with me. She also promised to bring them to the movies and visit family more often. Amelia was being strict for a reason, but always gave us something to offset her strict rules.

Haitian parents are very strict and are no strangers to giving beatings. They'd rather us cry now then they cry in the future due to bad behavior or someone hurting us. One thing my mom didn't believe in is slapping her children.

I was slapped one time, and it was because of my judgmental rude mouth to an adult. She did it so karma wouldn't get me. The person was also Haitian, and she didn't want any reason for a spiritual attack. Haitians and people of the world are very good with spiritual warfare. Their faith is strong. It is hard to tell who is who but sometimes you can feel their energy.

The twins went to watch cartoons after Amelia talked. Amelia started to make dinner and I was her assistant. I asked her why the twins needed me to go to Kat's house. Amelia said they were too young, and nobody loves your family like you. Amelia winked at me and said people are like oranges and the twins are too young and vulnerable to know about oranges.

We heard a little voice saying, "Who has oranges?" It was Princess being greedy. We started laughing at Princess as she stood there, confused, and waiting for an orange.

Dinner was delicious. We had stewed chicken, red beans with rice, and salad. I kept thinking about Rob. I wished he would go away. He was not from Newkirk and was sort of nerd-like. The relationship did not make sense to me, but what did I know, I was just a kid.

My mom told me not to judge a book by its cover. I even got into trouble for looking down at a man when I was seven-years old. My mom popped me in the mouth right in front of him. When we got home, Amelia explained to me how people and life are funny. "You never know who will help you when you need it. It might be the hustler on the corner or the old lady that never minds her own business. Do not let your attitude stand in the way of your blessings." All I knew was that I was going to miss seeing Slim. I didn't understand why she left when things were just starting to look good in her family. I didn't want to make things worse by asking. I figured she would tell me in time.

GRADUATION

G raduation came and I was excited for so many reasons. I was going to high school. I was both happy and sad at the same time. I was going to miss all the friends I had met and couldn't wait to get away from the people I didn't like.

I loved new beginnings. I already knew I wasn't going to see some of my friends anymore. We didn't live in the same neighborhood. I didn't like going to people's houses, so we only socialized in school.

The only person I wished could be around was Slim. I hadn't heard from her in months. She was always so optimistic about everything. I felt sad planning events without Slim. She had been happy despite her home life. Sometimes I think she needed everything to be alright. She reminded me of a beautiful, abused puppy.

Amelia was planning a small family gathering for my graduation. All my aunts and cousin were coming, as well as a few family friends. My grandmother, Eve, was coming from Haiti to attend my party.

I love Eve. All she did was travel since Pop Pop died. She was the most elegant woman I knew. She reminded me of Cecily Tyson in Hoodlum. Eve was always dressed to kill. Her makeup and hair were always flawless. She could bake and cook. You wouldn't expect her to be able to this; at first glance, she resembled and acted like royalty. She was wise, humble, loving, and a protector.

Eve small frame fooled people. She was the glue that kept the family together. She always came to us when she was needed and managed to make everything okay. Eve was sent away to Paris to be educated, but she was 100 percent Haitian at heart. Her ancestors were from Guinea;

they were kidnapped and brought to Haiti through the slave trade.

My family passed down stories from one generation to the other. They passed down stories to teach us about human nature, politics, love, struggles, and survival. We were proud of where we came from. We were proud that Haiti won their independence in 1804.

I loved the fact that I looked like Eve. I was her younger version without the loose soft curls and hazel eyes. Eve preferred to speak Creole with the family. She was fluent in French, English, and Spanish. Her presence was a gift in itself.

Kat was coming. Slim and Kat had attended all my family functions. This would be the first event that Slim would miss since I met her. They were used to my family and the Haitian culture. They knew the proper greetings and they heard the folktales. They were used to the loud laughter and music and they loved the exotic foods. Haitian functions are a site to see. The clothes, the music and the decorations were always high end.

The senior women would wear wigs, pearls, diamonds, rubies, and emeralds. The women's suits were always colorful. They wore colors like beige, light purple, pastel, light yellow, light blue, or all white.

The young ladies would wear form-fitting beautiful dresses, high heels, and big hair which had been set in rollers. Their makeup was usually flawless. They loved highlights in their hair. Haitian women get dressed to kill for special events because they usually dress pretty modestly compared to everyone else.

They shy away from American culture. Their goals

are to make a living and to take care of their families in the United States and the ones still living in Haiti. Haitians are the good girls of the Caribbean.

The teenage girls usually wear the same colors as their mother. They are like their mother's mini me. Their mothers usually wear form fitting dresses that are made by a seamstress. The little girls usually dress like a princess. They would wear puffy colorful dresses and lace stockings.

The older men would wear their best suits, a gold chain, and glasses. The younger men would wear dress pants, button down shirts and glasses. They would wear solid dark colors. It was a beautiful scene.

It didn't feel like Brooklyn during the function. It felt like another world. It was a joyful escape from responsibilities. There were usually a handful of Americans at our party. People brought along their American best friends, in-laws, coworkers, and their Asian or Caucasian boyfriend or girlfriend. Everyone usually spokes Creole. They would speak English if they noticed Americans were close by.

Haitians are great story tellers. They usually tell stories about Haiti and Lougawou. Sometimes they talk about their experiences in the United States. They told how people assumed they didn't speak English or didn't know how the system works. They love coming out on top while acting dumb. There is a lot of dancing.

The Haitian culture is complicated. They practiced the African ways and learned from the French. Haitians travel all over the world and retain their own culture and beliefs. Haitians are very proud of their history and culture. Their culture is very difficult for an outsider to understand. They are very spiritual by nature but understand science and use logic. I was so excited thinking about my graduation and my party.

My graduation was only five days away and my graduation party was six days away. I was counting down the days to freedom. The days were long, especially when I was in school. There wasn't any real work to be completed; everyone had already taken the city exams and knew what high school they were going to.

A few people were not graduating, but it had been expected. They hadn't come to school often, and when they did, they cut out early. They didn't do any schoolwork. As I walked down the hall, I saw strangers that had become friends and friends that had become strangers. I saw enemies that had become associates.

I think all the seniors had mixed emotions. I saw people laughing and crying in the hallways, classrooms, and cafeteria. Everyone was hugging each other. Everyone wanted to know where everyone else was going. They were forming new alliances for a new environment. This information turned enemies into friends the last few weeks of school. People were hugging and kissing each other and telling them how much they were going to miss each other.

I saw Keith and thought about how I used to love him. We played around a lot acting like we forgot what happened two years earlier. I sometimes caught myself staring at him, and sometimes I caught him staring at me. He was my first love and my first heartbreak. I promised myself never to talk to anyone in the same school that I attended.

Some days I was so over him while other days he stayed on my mind. It was torture when we did play around and pretend to fight. I'd catch him smelling my hair like he used to. In the past, that usually led to a kiss but now there was no kiss, just an extra tight hug and our face rub. Keith and I were not going to the same high school so I doubted we would see each other much.

We didn't see Janelle anymore either. She had gotten pregnant by a high school kid and was sent back to Trinidad after giving birth. West Indians sometimes send their kids home for bad behavior and pregnancy.

The day of my graduation was hot and muggy. It was weird to see some of my classmate's family members. I never really thought about their families or home life.

I saw this kid named Mike that used to get picked on. He was being hugged by his parents and younger siblings. His family was beautiful, and so was he underneath his bifocals. It was like I was seeing him for the first time. I was never mean to him because he was nice, and I was not into that. I saw this other kid named James trying to distance himself from his drug-addicted mother. He was very popular at school and she looked so proud of him.

I walked up to James, just to compliment his mother on her outfit. She quickly kissed him on his cheek and started saying how proud she was of him. I could see why he worked so hard in school. I felt bad that he felt uncomfortable by his mom's presence.

James reminded me of my cousin Tracey. She used to be embarrassed by her mother, Nene. James's mother reminded me of my Aunt Nene a little. She had beautiful features. My Aunt Nene makes me look at some people different. I introduced him to my family, and he gave them a huge hug. I winked at James. He started showing more affection towards his mother. My mother invited them to my party. I was surprised but Amelia must have noticed what I was trying to do.

Everyone was excited about my graduation party. The party was for my graduation, but it was really for all of us. My aunts, Eve, and my cousin, Paula, were helping my mom cook. Paula was actually married to my mom's cousin, Dave. She made herself a fixture at all our family events and she was overly nice.

Paula and Dave were the only ones spending the night because they lived in Queens. They stayed in the spare bedroom and their children stayed in my room. I was kind of upset because this arrangement meant that Eve had to stay with my aunts until they left. Paula's children loved their dad, but they were afraid of her. She always threatened to kill them through voodoo.

I could never trust someone whose own children believed they would kill them. It didn't matter how much they smiled and laughed. My graduation theme colors were red and white. The decorations, cake, and the clothes that we would be wearing were red and white. I had told Kat so she can wear the same colors too. She was my best friend.

My dress was white with a red waist belt. It came down to my calves. It was form-fitting but not tight. The dress had a small split up the right side and was strapless. I wore a rose broach with gold rose leaves on the left side of my chest. I was so excited because this was the first time that I had gone to a hair salon. I went to a Dominican spot in Flatbush.

My hair was styled in an up-do with curls. It was beautiful. I felt grown up and received plenty of compliments. I remember one weird compliment that was given to me, but I just smiled and said thank you. This older lady said, "She is pretty for a dark-skinned girl and look at all that hair." I thought it was normal to have a head full of hair and I was born beautiful. I noticed some of the neighborhood boys were looking at me like Keith did. I jabbed them in the arms so they would know I didn't change, and our friendships would not change either.

I finally made it home and Princess hugged and kissed me. She then said she wanted her hair to look like mine. We all laughed and told her that her hair looked pretty in bubbles and barrettes. I helped with the decorations. I was so happy. I couldn't wait for the gifts, the cake, the dancing, and seeing most of my family.

It's always fun and I always learn something new about someone. I usually sat in silence while other people spoke, talking freely and forgetting I was even there. I got to hear how people really are. I figured them out most of the time. Some people don't change, they just hid that they were older. It was going to be hard to be invisible since it was my party.

The party was supposed to start at 7:00 p.m., but we were still arranging the food. The guests started arriving as we were setting things up. We were playing Kompa music. My family and my best friend were there. I felt like everything was perfect.

James and his mother showed up. This was their first time to a Haitian event. My mom and I made them feel welcome. They enjoyed the food. The apartment door was left open so we didn't have to keep going to the door and people could feel welcome. I was excited about the envelopes I saw people give to my mother for me.

Around 8:30 p.m., I saw Keith walk in. I was surprised because I hadn't invited him. I quickly looked at Kat and she gave me a devilish grin. I smiled. That is why she was my best friend.

Keith came by himself. Lately he was always by himself. Lee had been expelled from Ditmas earlier that year because of one of his pranks that went too far. I think it is funny how life removes negative people from your world. Keith stayed close to Kat and I. Tracey was hanging out with me. Everyone was enjoying themselves until Paula came and gave me a devilish look, as if I had done something wrong at my party. I acted like I didn't see her, but Kat started laughing. Paula realized I was ignoring her, and she walked away, appearing upset. I brushed it off and didn't think twice of it.

Tracey and Nene had similar red and white outfits. The showstoppers were Amelia, Grandma Eve, and my aunts. They looked like royalty. Eve looked like a queen. Everyone complimented her on her timeless beauty and style. Our guests were happy to see Eve. I was happy to see her. My friends were even mesmerized by her grace and elegance.

Grandma Eve's aura demands attention and respect.

She doesn't strive to get attention; it just happens, unlike my cousin Paula.

Paula had gone out and bought red and white outfits to match the theme colors. Her daughter's hair style had been done in a style similar to mine. I didn't say anything, but I was upset. She was making the day about her and her family. I didn't know why my mom couldn't see that she was bad news.

I think it's the love for her cousin. He is a soft, gentle, timid man that grew up with her. My mom felt relaxed around him. The environment was relaxed, and everyone was happy. I was able to do things that I usually couldn't. I was able to drink Cremas. This is a Haitian coconut drink with alcohol.

The party went smoothly. Everyone enjoyed themselves. Keith offered to help put things away, but Paula was quick to say we didn't need any help. I took it as a reason to chill. I wasn't helping anymore.

I was frustrated by this woman, but in my culture, it would have been rude to say anything. Paula picked up a handful of everything and put it in a plastic bag when no one was looking. Everyone took plates to eat but this wasn't the case. She treated it as if it were garbage, but then put it in a cabinet. I acted like I didn't see it, but I thought it was weird. The party ended around 1:00 a.m. Kat spent the night.

Kat and I were the only ones up and we thought we heard something. It sounded like the apartment door opening. We decided to investigate, and quietly walked towards the door just in case it was a burglar.

The door was unlocked, so we realized that someone

had left the apartment. We looked out and caught the backside of the person leaving, so we decided to follow them. We followed the person from a safe distance, and realized the person was my cousin, Paula.

Paula reached Flatbush with all the stores and heavy traffic, and she dropped the plastic bag she had filled up at the party in the middle of the street.

Once we saw what she did, we turned around and ran back to beat her to the house. We also had no business being outside this late or early in the morning.

Once we got to the house, I checked the cabinet just to make sure it was the same bag. It was, so we hurried up to my room. We couldn't talk about it because her children were in my room. However, the next morning we went to Kat's house for privacy to discuss the party experience in private.

I thought Paula was weird before, but this behavior sealed the deal. I know for a fact it was something spiritual that this woman was doing at my party. I knew it was not good because she was being sneaky, and it wasn't her place to do whatever she had done.

Kat advised me to tell my mother. Then we quickly changed the subject to how much fun we had. I thanked Kat again for inviting Keith. Keith and James were getting along at my party, although they ran in different circles in school. I guess they had no choice since they were the only two boys from Ditmas.

I personally think James and Keith are a better fit as friends. They both had dreams and goals. Keith was more into sports and James was more into science, but they were committed, and both planned on being successful. Failure was not an option for them. Kat joked about how I had two boyfriends at my party. I hadn't even noticed that James liked me. I was too busy playing host and trying to have fun at the same time. I never thought about James that way. I never thought of anyone, other than Keith, in that way.

The last day of school was emotional because it was the official goodbye. We went to pick up our yearbooks and report cards. They announced people who had the highest scores in the citywide tests. They also gave out awards that hadn't been presented during the graduation ceremony.

I saw James because he was in my homeroom class. He approached me as soon as I walked in. He was telling the other kids how cool and different Haitians are. They were excited hearing about it and wanted to know why I didn't invite them. I told them I didn't think they would be interested. I actually saw my culture through someone else's eyes, and it was beautiful.

I found out that day that James would be spending his summer at a summer science program. I acted excited for him, but I wanted to hang out. I already knew Keith was going to summer football camp. It made me start thinking how they already had their life planned and were working towards their goals.

I started thinking about my future. I always had good grades, but I never really thought about my adult life. I felt behind. The only good part about hearing this was that I didn't have to choose between James and Keith, and I had the whole summer to myself.

I decided at that moment that I would marry a man

similar to Keith and James. I loved the fact that they knew what they wanted and were willing to work towards their goal. Their future successes would not be by mistake. I wanted my future husband to be confident and able to do things without my help. I know it sounded selfish, but I didn't want someone who needed me for the material things. I wanted someone who needed me emotionally.

Kat and I had big plans. We weren't sure of the exact details, but we had plans. Kat and I just knew we were grown; we were going to high school. We had our whole lives ahead of us. We had more freedom and a bigger allowance. Flatbush was ours that summer. We outgrew 21st and Newkirk and wanted to see all of Brooklyn.

In reality, we wanted to meet new boys. We played and argued with the boys around us as if they were our brothers, even if they did not want to be. I am not going to lie--we were flirts. We kissed the boys and literally watched them cry. We even dated older boys. It was pure fun and excitement to tease them and we then watched them trying to please us. Kat and I learned that a man will act differently in front of his friends. We even divided them up into four different types.

Type A was the smooth, laid-back type. He was a control freak and calculative. He also can be controlled. The key is to ask him for things behind closed doors and always make it appear that it was his idea.

Type B is narcissistic. He's flashy and always had to prove that he was capable of everything. So, with Type B, you had to ask him or challenge him in front of other people.

Type C guys were the lost causes. These men were

so tampered with or damaged by their mothers, friends, society, or life, that they were incapable of being happy. We would cut them off like a cancer.

Type D boys were the boys we all wanted because they were fun with great qualities. They were cool. They were the ones that appeared to have it all together with no emotional baggage or scars.

It was kind of dangerous flirting with all these boys, but we were smart enough not to have them live close to each other, get attacked, or have sex with them. We also practiced the buddy system. We never left each other alone or let the guys outnumber us. It just didn't look right.

We would sometimes bring other associates with us to even out the numbers, but never around the guys that we really liked or were baller-type dudes. We were always on the go and always made our curfew. We never stayed in one place too long. We stayed on the trains or dollar vans or we walked. We had fun traveling.

Kat and I felt like the block superstars. People always wanted to know where we were going or coming from. Coming from one of our escapades one night, we noticed that Slim was standing in front of the building and we ran up to her. Something about her seemed different.

Slim was dressed really nice, but her eyes looked extra sad. She also looked like she had gained some weight; something I thought was impossible for Slim. I would not have been able to imagine a heavier Slim. We told her she looked nice and she did. Kat was always the bold one, so she blurted out, "What is wrong with you Slim?" Slim looked like she wanted to cry, so Kat quickly suggested that we go to her apartment.

Kat's house was more private, as usual. She was the only child living in her home and her mom and stepdad came home from work later than my mom. It felt like old times and we were having one of our serious emergency meetings.

When we got to Kat's room, Slim burst into tears. She reminded me of how we had become friends' years before. I asked slim what was wrong. "Is someone bothering you? What is going on?" Kat and I just kept spitting questions at her.

Slim whispered that she was pregnant. The room was suddenly silent. It didn't make sense to us because Slim was a good girl, like us. We had all promised each other that we were not going to even think about sex until we were 18-years old and, even then, he would have to be extra special or something.

I felt like my heart was broken, so I asked her if she loved him. Slim started crying even harder. We both went and hugged her. She was only 16 and we were 13-years old. This problem was bigger than all of us. I told Slim she didn't have to talk about it until she was ready.

Slim turned around and asked if she could spend the week at my house. I thought that was weird because her mom lived right across the hall, but I told her I would have to ask Amelia for the first night. We decided we should have a slumber party at Kat's house first.

It almost felt like old times. It was the same, but also different. I went to my house to ask Amelia if I could spend the night at Kat's house. Amelia said I could, and the twins were coming too.

Then I asked if Slim could spend the week with us. My mom's face turned red. I didn't understand her anger and immediately regretted asking her about Slim. I never saw Amelia react this way over two questions. Amelia asked me why she needed to spend the week at our house. I quickly asked, "Mommy, what is wrong? I thought you liked Slim?"

Amelia's whole demeanor changed, and I suddenly realized that she was not mad at me or Slim. I also realized that Slim was waiting for Kat and me to come home in front of the building today.

Amelia told me that Slim could spend the week with us after she spoke to Nelly. She wanted me to come with her. I was shocked because Amelia never knocked on Nelly's door before. After ringing Nelly's bell, Rob answered the door. Amelia asked Rob if Nelly was home, and Rob led us to the living room.

It was a house that I'd been in less than a dozen times, but I could still describe every detail of that home. The living room was dark but neat with old furniture. The couches smelled like an old astray that no matter how many times you washed it; the smell never left. Nelly was a chain smoker. Nelly was sleeping on the couch, but quickly sat up and tried to straighten out her appearance when she saw Amelia.

Nelly was barely dressed. She had on a cream-colored polyester nightgown with blue lace ribbon. It was stained. You could tell that it was once white but had changed color because it was not washed properly. Nelly's hair was slicked down into a small ponytail. Her face always looked greasy, no matter what season or time of the day you saw her.

Nelly was brown skinned with very strong afro-centric features. She could be pretty if she took care of herself. You could tell that she used to be pretty, but years of drugs and alcohol destroyed her looks. The inside of her lips were red from drinking. Her eyes were always red, and she looked tired all the time. Even if she stopped using drugs today, you would be able tell she was once an addict. Nelly had addiction behavior that she was not willing to let go.

Nelly had a lump on the left side of her face. It looked like it had been there for a couple of days. She smiled at Amelia but had a puzzled look on her face. Amelia never knocked on Nelly's door. Amelia greeted Nelly. My mom was always respectful, even when she was angry. Amelia was always calm and soft-spoken, but very direct.

Amelia asked Nelly if Slim could spend the week at our house. Nelly's whole demeanor changed. Nelly was shocked that we were talking about Slim. She looked like she saw a ghost.

Nelly quickly asked where Slim was and what had she been telling us. Amelia said, "Nothing, but is there anything she should be telling us? Is there something wrong? I have never known Slim to be a bad child that got into trouble." Nelly just stared and looked lost and that's when Rob started rambling.

"You do not know Slim; she is wild, she's running wild with a gang of girls, being hot. She's a bad influence on her younger siblings and she is trying to ruin the only good thing her mom has had for years. If she wants to be grown, she can go be grown in the streets." Calmly, Amelia told Rob that she was speaking to the child's mother.

Amelia turned to Nelly and said, "Do you feel that Slim should be living in the streets? You are giving up on your daughter. Oh, I see, you have a man and now Slim has to go. You can't have another woman in the house.

It is making sense now. Rob moved in and all of a sudden Slim is hot and out of control. Even if she was hot, it isn't like you didn't push her to go looking for love." And then, out of nowhere, Rob shouted: "Mind your business, you stupid Haitian chink." Amelia looked at him and smiled.

Everyone was looking at her with a puzzled expression. Except me--I was scared. I had seen that reaction before, with the twin's dad. Amelia's smile turned into a chuckle. She asked Rob, "So, you're the prize? You are supposed to be the man in the house. Sal lope, vagabond sal malpropte.

I see how you help this family. Slim was thrown out and Nelly is your free punching bag. Do you feel strong, important, and manly? Well Rob, you are nothing. You are less than a man; you prey on an addicted woman and her kids. As for me, if you see a bitch, slap a bitch!" Rob was ready to attack Amelia, but Nelly quickly ran in front of him and begged him not to touch her.

Nelly was crying as she said, "Stop, you don't know who she is; you don't know what she can do." Amelia did not yell, flinch, or make a move while all of this was going on. Even the smirk on her face didn't change. But it wasn't the smirk that gave away her deviant intentions, it was her eyes.

It was the way her dark, marble eyes narrowed, never losing sight of her prey. It was the look of a lioness protecting her cubs. It was the look of an insane person, fixated on one individual out of a crowd of 100. Nelly got Rob to apologize and continued talking to my mom. But the damage was done. I didn't know it, but the damage had been done long before we went to Nelly's house. Amelia just wanted confirmation.

Amelia looked at Nelly and said, "You never did answer my question. Can Slim live with me until everything gets sorted out?" Nelly didn't even look at Amelia when she whispered that she could have her.

Amelia opened Nelly's door and nudged me, and we walked out and went into our apartment. I was curious what Nelly meant when she told Rob that she didn't know who Amelia was. I was also confused about why he called my mom a Haitian Chink.

We never broadcast an Asian part of the family. We never spoke about Pop Pop. His family still lives in Haiti. They didn't want to leave the comfort of Haiti. They had the good life there. They had their business and properties. I didn't ask Amelia what Nelly met, and I definitely didn't want to ask Nelly. We just walked back to the apartment in silence.

The minute Amelia got back into her apartment; the tears began running down her cheeks. I ran to hug Amelia, promising to take care of Rob for her. Amelia hugged me so tight. Then she asked me if anyone had ever tried to touch me. I told her no. She made me swear to tell her if anyone tried to hurt me or the twins.

Amelia gave me one of those famous Haitian speeches,

reminding me that I would be her baby until infinity. She reminded me that the world was a cruel place, and everyone doesn't see me as she sees me. She will forever see me as her first born baby. Amelia said, "I need to talk to you about men. Let me be exact; some men will try their hardest to get into your pants. They do not care how young you are. They will promise you the world and give you gifts, but, in the end, it is all a game.

The most important thing is to know we all make mistakes. Don't ever let your mistakes own you. Own your mistakes first. Once you own anything, you can do as you please." What Amelia said really didn't make sense to me, but I always remembered her words.

After our conversation, Amelia quickly got on the phone with her sisters. They were all coming to the house. Amelia sent the twins with me to Kat's house. I knew it was because she didn't want us to hear their conversation.

When we got to Kat's house, Slim was still sleeping and Kat was watching a video music box. I gave Kat a look that told her something big had just gone down. She and I were able to read each other's facial expressions so well it was down-right scary. We snuck into the living room while the twins were hypnotized by the music videos.

I told Kat how my mom had gone to ask Nelly if Slim could spend the week and it turned into an argument. Kat was shocked that Nelly argued with Amelia. I had to quickly correct her and told her it was Rob. It didn't make sense to any of us.

Then I told Kat that I thought Nelly gave Slim to Amelia. Kat was like, "What do you mean? What happened? What was said?" So, I told her that Amelia had asked if Slim could stay with us and Nelly whispered, "You can have her." Kat and I were so involved in the conversation that we did not notice that Slim was standing there, crying, until it was too late.

Slim sounded like a wounded puppy and looked completely defeated. She had heard the whole conversation. Slim just walked to where we were sitting and laid her head on my lap and her legs on Kat's lap. Slim whispered, "Nelly doesn't want me anymore?" We didn't know what to say.

It was obvious to Kat and me that Nelly had never wanted her. Nelly never did anything for Slim. In fact, Slim did more for Nelly. But we did think it was weird that Nelly was ready to let Slim go now.

What made Rob different from any other man? I patted Slim on the back while she was crying. She asked me if I minded that she would be living with me. Of course, I said no. I always wanted an older sister. Then Slim asked if Amelia knew she was pregnant. I told her "No," because I hadn't told her.

That was the one thing we never did--tell on each other's secrets. I wasn't going to start now. Slim said, "Good, because I am not keeping it.

Slim don't know how but was determined to get rid of it." When I asked her about the father, she said he was the one that ruined her life. She told me the baby was Rob's. I blurted out "Why?" and "How?" and "That's your mom's boyfriend."

Kat gave me a look, and I knew I had said something stupid. That is when I started putting the pieces together.

I had heard stories about men being perverts. This was the first time I knew the victim personally.

This was horrible. I cried every time I thought of what Rob did to Slim. She was a tiny thing. She never had any real support from her mother and Rob knew that. Then they had the nerve to kick her out like she was nothing. I knew Slim was hurting. I thought she was the bravest person I knew. I knew for a fact she was waiting for us. She didn't have a home at Nelly's house.

Slim and Kat wanted to know everything that happened. I mentioned how I was confused when Nelly told Rob that he didn't know who Amelia was. Kat and Slim looked at each other. I knew right then that they knew something they weren't telling me. I gave them the look and Kat said she thought I knew. I quickly asked them about what I was supposed to know. I was confused again. Slim sat up and asked me if I really didn't know.

Slim started hinting that is was about my family. That was the reason people were so nice or stayed out of Amelia's way. They didn't want to get on her bad side and reap the repercussions. I thought they were going to talk about my dad. That was weird for people to be afraid of a ghost. He was dead. I wasn't going to offer any information. I only knew bits and pieces of my dad's lifestyle anyway.

Then Slim asked me if I had ever heard of Chinaman. I was like, who hadn't heard of Chinaman. He was an Asian drug lord. He was never in jail and was never indicted, but he controlled the drugs that ran through the five borrows. Everyone worked with him in one form of another. He was dangerous. He was like a ghost. It was unheard of--a Chinese man working with an African American and a west Indian to deal drugs.

This was one of the reasons why the NYPD couldn't imagine he was the mastermind of his drug empire. If he had been working in Chinatown with other Chinese people, he would have been apprehended or at least suspected.

He didn't belong in Chinatown despite his Asian DNA. He was west Indian and didn't speak a lick of Chinese. He was a black man in his heart and soul and understood the culture. He was also an older man. He never got his hands dirty.

Kat blurted out that "the word around the street is that Chinaman is your grandfather." I had to sit down. I was shocked. My Pop Pop was a normal, loving grandfather. He wouldn't hurt a soul.

I was hurt because no one had told about him. My best friends didn't even tell me. That's when I heard the voice of my great grandmother whispering in my ear that a secret is never shared by two.

I stayed silent and didn't react to the new information. I thought we three had told each other everything. I told them everything, even when it was about them. I kept my anger inside because I knew Slim was going through some horrible things. This was also something I needed to discuss with my mother.

I acted like I was shocked and excited. They wanted to continue to talk about it, but I told them they knew more than I do. My cousin Tracey came and knocked on the door for me.

I was happy to see Tracey. She saved me from

exploding. I didn't know how long I could have kept my cool. I left with the twins and Slim wanted to stay at Kat's house for a little while. I knew it was because they were going to talk about me. I was okay with that because we did it to each other all the time to spare each other's feelings and help solve our problems.

Tracey knew something was wrong the minute she saw my face. She was only 10-years old at the time, but she was very sharp. She asked me what was wrong and who did she have to beat up. I looked at her beautiful young face and said nothing and hugged her tightly.

Tracey made me realize that my mom was trying to protect me like we tried to protect her. She didn't need to know this. I also know how she felt when other people told her information about Aunt Nene.

Amelia asked where Slim was. I told her she wanted to stay at Kat's house for a little while. Amelia had this confused look on her face. She wanted all of us here. Amelia knew that Slim needed structure. Slim would have to follow the same rules that I followed.

Amelia needed to speak to Slim, but she spoke to me by myself. She asked how I felt about Slim living here. I was kind of mad at Slim, so I gave Amelia a dry okay. My mom explained that she had to bring Slim to the police precinct to make a report and make things official. She didn't want any trouble with children and youth services, nor jeopardize her own children.

The next morning, she spoke to Slim and told her that they had to file a police report explaining what had happened to her. Slim told Amelia that she was pregnant. I was so happy I had not been included in that conversation.

Amelia took Slim to the 70th Police Precinct. She and Slim filed a report and provided information on Rob and Nelly. The police said they would investigate it and gave Amelia information regarding family court and children and youth services.

Amelia started working on the paperwork immediately. She wanted to make everything official. She didn't want any surprises. Amelia took the day off to take care of everything. I was happy and sad at the same time. I was used to being the only older girl in the house. I was also still processing what they had said about Pop Pop. I didn't get any alone time to speak to Amelia about it. The freedom I had for the summer was short lived.

A week went by and nothing happened. It was like the incident never occurred. There was no word from the detectives from sex crimes. Slim, Kat, and I were not allowed to play in the hallway.

Kat's mother and Amelia spoke about what happened to Slim. They wanted to make sure we were safe, so they put us on a buddy system. All of a sudden, the problems I had in the past and the problems I had in school seem so petty.

My whole world had changed. I looked at everything differently--the world and people. This was the second time in my life that I didn't feel safe, and I didn't like it. I was angry and felt like a caged animal. I loved my summers. I knew Amelia could handle things, but she was taking too long. I couldn't question her about what she was going to do, because she was trying to shelter me from what the family could do and how they handled things. I didn't want to imagine what the family could do.

Kat, Slim, and I were frustrated. We made up a game about what we thought should happen to Rob. I wanted to add Nelly, but Slim wasn't ready for that game. We decided we wanted him to be scared, just like us. We wanted him to be afraid of Newkirk. He wasn't even from Newkirk, so he could easily go back to the Bronx where he came from. We wanted things to return to normal--the way it used to be. The reality was that things would never go back to the way they were. The damage and changes were done. You either accept change or become extinct.

We decided we had to do something to forget about things, so we went for a walk. We started to walk towards the junction, but that got boring. We decided to visit Kat's cousin who lived in the Vandevear project.

Slim started complaining about being hungry and her feet hurting. This was unusual for Slim, as she would walk to the end of the earth if it was not after curfew. I guess being pregnant changes people. We stopped at a pizza store to eat and take a break. We stayed for about 30 minutes and then continued our walk to the Vandevear project.

As we walked up Foster Avenue, we heard someone called out for Slim. I was about to stop, but Slim said to keep walking and started to speed walk. Three boys came up to us. This light-skinned kid, who also happened to be the biggest one, grabbed Slim by her shirt asking where the fuck she had been.

Kat and I ran to her defense and tried to get his arm off of her. We were quickly pushed to the ground. We didn't know what hit us; things were getting bad really quickly. I was angry and confused. No one hits me; who the hell did these pieces of shit think they were?

Slim quickly came to our defense. She started begging for them to leave us alone. Slim called the largest of the three boys, "Looney." She said, "Please, they are my little cousins, let them go and I promise I will stay." By then I was crying, and I shouted out, "Mommy is expecting you to come home. I can't leave you here." Looney smiled and was like, see they don't want to go. Let them come in and we can be one big, happy family.

Kat and I looked at each other because we knew exactly what Looney met. Our faces went blank as we stood there frozen and scared. Things were happening too fast. We just stood there, watching Slim crying, and begging to get things right. We looked at Looney's friends, staring at us like we were cake. My head was heavy, my stomach was knotting up, and I couldn't feel my arms and legs. I felt like I was in a bad nightmare and couldn't wake up. I was praying.

There were people around, but they acted like they didn't see anything. I was thinking of Newkirk. This wouldn't happen to me in Newkirk.

I guess it's true that everyone is a big shot on their block. Then I thought about Amelia. She would kill anyone that would touch me, but she's not here. No one was here. I threw myself on the ground and decided I wasn't walking anywhere! The two boys were trying to say something, but I couldn't hear a word. The next thing I knew, someone picked me up and held me tight. I started to fight, until I heard him say "Sherry sak passé."

When I looked up, it was my older cousin, Reginald.

I told him, "Mien pa conne. Se mache mappe mache avec mon ami vagabond sal viene attacke mien. Vagabond sal vle pu allez avec yo." I had my arms wrapped tightly around his waist as I was crying and explaining what had happened to us.

Reginald asked Looney in English what happened. Looney stood there confused and scared. Looney was shocked that Reginald knew us. I blurted out that they attacked us and wouldn't let us go home. Reginald looked at our scared and angry faces and told us to get in the car. Looney and his goons said nothing. All their tough talk ended. They didn't try to stop us. They stood there in silence. It was a miracle that my cousin came to our aid. Looney still had ahold of Slim, like she was his prized possession.

His goons were sitting on the steps of his house. I yelled out to Reginald that my mom was expecting Slim to come home because she lived with us. Reginald ordered Kat and me to get in the car. This time his voice sounded like he was upset. We got in the car.

Reginald walked over to Looney and they walked to the side to talk. Slim stood there, scared. I couldn't understand why she didn't run into the car as this was a good opportunity. I couldn't imagine what control this man had on my friend. I was crying in the car because I didn't want Slim to stay. I didn't want her to be around those bullies.

Reginald and Looney spoke for a couple of minutes, then shook hands, and Looney told Slim to get in the car. Slim looked back as if she felt sorry for Looney and got into the car. I was confused at the way Slim looked at Looney.

I wanted to get out of there and never look back. I had enough. I felt like my childhood was leaving; my whole world was changing too fast. I felt fear. I never feared anyone before. I never really experienced true danger before. Then Reginald got into the car and we drove off. The ride was silent. Reginald asked us if we wanted something to eat. Basically, Reginald wanted to know what was going on. The only person that really knew was Slim. We decided that we wanted Popeye's on Empire Blvd.

Reginald was only 17 but stood about 6 foot 5 inches. He wore his hair in a ponytail. People often mistook him for being an American Indian or being born in India. He drove a black Maxima; which Grandpapa gave him for his birthday. He was Aunt Dalia's first born. He was also Grandpapa's favorite and that meant a lot. Anything Reginald wanted; Reginald got.

Reginald knew everyone, but only had one best friend, whose name was Rickey. They grew up together and they both were into sports and girls.

Reginald drove us to Popeye's, and we ordered what we wanted. He was always treating me and the younger children in the family when he came around. I wasn't really hungry, but I was not ready to go home. This was the worst thing I had experienced in my life. I knew I was lucky that day.

Slim, on the other hand, was born unlucky. She was born into the wrong family, to the worst mother, and now was being exposed to the wrong people. I felt sorry for her. She was like a puppy being kicked around for no reason.

Reginald turned to Slim and asked how she ended up being involved with Looney. We all looked at Slim. Slim started crying hysterically, but before she could say anything, Kat blurted out, "Shut the hell up. I am tired of you crying and expecting people to feel sorry for you. You do stupid things and you could have gotten me hurt. You knew it was dangerous to be around Rodgers Avenue, but you didn't warn us.

I am not trying to judge you, but if you want to deal with crazy people go ahead. Paris and I did not have to walk down that block. Heck, we can't even walk down our own block because of you."

Slim was trying to say she was sorry, but Kat was crying and full of rage. Kat said, "You are sorry! It's no wonder Nelly don't want you." By this time, tears were running from all our eyes. I sat there in silence looking at Kat and Slim.

Kat suddenly stop venting, once she realized that Slim didn't say anything. She just sat there crying, looking down. This wasn't like Slim; she had a smart mouth. Lately, though, she just took in everything that people threw at her. Whatever happened to her with Nelly, Rob, Looney, and whoever else she encountered these past few months must have broken her. Then Kat did something I had never heard her do before; she apologized to Slim and gave her a hug. Kat doesn't apologize to anyone!

Reginald broke the silence by asking Slim what she was going to do about this baby. "Looney said it is his baby, and you were living with him and just disappeared one day."

My mouth dropped when I heard that. Slim was too young to be shacking up. Now it made sense. Slim must have been through so much when she was on her own. I don't know why she didn't come to us sooner. I didn't ask but it hurt my heart just thinking about it.

I never thought of what she was doing or how she was surviving. It must have been hard for her to return to Newkirk after what Rob had done to her. I felt sorry for her and how she was able to muster up a smile when she had first seen us. She had been waiting for us. In actuality, we were what she had left of her childhood. And, although she didn't mean to, Slim took a little of our childhood when she came back.

Slim told us that she didn't know what she was going to do with her baby and the situation. I looked at Reggie; he must have known what I was going to ask because he said he would not tell Amelia anything, but only if we promised to stay away from Rodgers Avenue. He didn't have to worry about Kat and me going there, but we all looked at Slim for a response.

Slim agreed too. Reggie brought us home. He came in, of course, to say hi to my mom and the twins. The twins loved Reggie. He was like a superstar to them!

I thought about what happened all night. I imagined how hard it must have been for Slim to live with Looney. Slim also had a secret that only the family knew. That is something we do well--keeping secrets, no matter how angry we may get at each other.

Kat wanted to hurt Slim tonight, but she kept her

mouth shut about Rob raping Slim and getting her pregnant. It was not Looney's baby. Rob was the reason we could no longer play outside. He was the reason Amelia called a family meeting and why we went to Vandavear to get away.

Rob was the reason that Slim met Looney and why we had to be rescued from him and his crew today. None of this would have ever happened if Rob hadn't moved to Newkirk. None of this would have happened if Nelly wasn't so irresponsible and desperate.

The more I thought about it, the angrier I got. Slim was just a kid like me. She shouldn't have to carry all those burdens. And now, Kat and I were thrown into this bullshit. This was not fair; it was not right! I wanted things to go back to the way they used to be--before things got out of hand.

Everyone thought I was too young to remember what happened to the twin's father and who did it. I was young, but I remembered the meeting. The streets still talk, and Aunt Nene told me he was the reason she suffered over the years. I saw it all happening again.

I woke up early the next day and went to knock on Kat's door. I didn't even bother to change from my pajamas to walk across the hall. I didn't really have to knock because Kat was expecting me. I opened the door and walked to the back of the apartment into Kat's room.

I wasn't prepared for the terrifying seen. Rob was hovered over Kat's half-dressed body. I quickly jumped on him and attacked him. He pushed me to the floor and continued to attack Kat. I threw a lamp at him, but he just turned around and grinned at me. Kat lay there, semiconscious, and this beast of a man who was twice her size continued to brutally assault her.

I felt helpless, so I ran out the room to get Amelia. I was running for the front door, but it suddenly closed, and Nelly was guarding the door. She didn't say a word, but her actions, eyes, and facial expressions spoke for her. She was not going to let me leave.

Kat was never supposed to wake up and me leaving this apartment was not part of the plan. Nelly knew how sick and violent Rob was, and she was okay with it. In fact, she was just like him in that she accepted it and even helped him all along. She stood by him and all of his grossness.

I quickly understood how Slim felt and saw the horror that was happening to Kat. If I didn't get out of there, I would be next. I ran straight for Nelly, swinging my arms with all my might, letting out all the anger and fear I had inside of me. I grabbed a hold of her head and kept banging it on the door.

Then I remembered that the goal was to go and get help. I couldn't take Rob on by myself. I pushed Nelly to the floor and reached for the door and opened it. I was running out and something grabbed my leg. I was falling down in slow motion. I could see my door, but I couldn't get to it.

I was in such shock that I couldn't even scream. I closed my eyes and put my arms out to break my fall. I felt a sharp pain on my right elbow. When I opened my eyes, I was on the floor in my bedroom. This had all been a dream. It felt so real. I was glad it was just a bad dream.

I snuck into the living room to call Kat, just to make

sure she was okay. I didn't want Slim to know about my nightmare. We needed to do something, quick. I told Kat that I was going to be at her house by noon. I knew that Slim usually took her first nap around this time. I would leave her a note so she wouldn't worry.

I wasn't angry at Slim, but I didn't think she would be able to handle our conversation or our plans to take care of things. Slim had given us some guidelines about getting older, but just like her, we had changed. We liked to think our way out of problems, but right now Slim was too weak and emotional.

We had realized the night before that Slim had no fight left in her. In fact, she had been defeated once Rob touched her. Even if she had not become pregnant, she should not have run. Rob is the one that should have left... in handcuffs. Her life had gotten worse since that day, and now it was spilling over to ours. It was getting messy, and I hated messes.

Kat felt worse because she kind of tolerated Slim. She loved Slim, but her patience was wearing thin. I went to the store and then went to Kat's house. Kat was still upset. It was bad enough that we had to deal with Rob, but now we had to deal with Looney too. We knew Slim hated Rob, but we weren't sure how she felt about Looney.

Kat almost lost it. She screamed that she didn't give a flying fuck about Looney or Rob. Kat hardly ever cursed unless she was angry, even among our peers. Both of them were a threat. I could live without ever seeing either one of them again. They needed to be the ones stressing. The question was how to arrange it so that Slim was not physically involved. Whatever we were to do, we had to do it quickly as we didn't want this horrible situation to last all summer.

I told Kat about my dream. We sat there and thought about everything. On one hand, we had Rob--who raped Slim and got her pregnant. On the other hand, we had Looney--who was controlling and crazy but thought Slim was carrying his baby; he appeared to care for Slim. Rob was just damage; Looney was a blessing in disguise.

We decided that we had to pay Looney a visit. It was dangerous, but it was our best chance to get rid of Rob. We planned to go there in a few days, and we were going to ride our bikes this time.

We made our way to Rodgers Avenue around 1:00 p.m. This was the time that summer school let out, and parents would be walking their children home from getting free summer lunches. We wanted a crowd around. Looney was on the block with Hammer and Blade. I couldn't stand them, but I had to do what needed to be done.

They noticed us before we even spoke. We stayed on the street and on our bikes. Kat signaled for Looney to come closer. Looney looked confused, but since he didn't want to look scared in front of his friends, he walked over. I was glad that his goons didn't follow him.

The first thing that Looney wanted to know was how Slim was doing. I was thinking, so, the beast has feelings. I told him that she was doing fine, and she was at my house. She sleeps a lot because she is pregnant.

Looney put a smirk on his face when he heard that. He was proud that he was going to be a father. I was thinking, that was the lie Slim had to make up for food and shelter.

I told him that Slim didn't like to come outside anymore. My mom didn't want her coming out much.

That statement alone raised Looney's curiosity, and he quickly asked why. Kat was better at telling stories, so she took over and explained why. "Slim doesn't like coming outside for the same reason she left her mother's house."

Looney looked confused and I could tell Slim had never told him the whole story. So, Kat told Looney that Slim was afraid of her mother's boyfriend, Rob, that lived in our building. He could figure out the rest. I noticed a vein popping in the middle of his head. He started ranting about how no girl of his would be afraid of any man on this earth.

Hammer and Blade moved closer to find out what was going on because, by now, Looney looked like he was ready to fight. We acted like we were going to leave, but Looney quickly asked us where we were going. I told him we only came here to let him know how Slim was doing because he was the father of her unborn child. I also told him that she was one of my best friends and I wasn't there to broadcast her business to a crowd.

Looney signaled for his goons to move back. I was surprised that they took commands, almost like dogs. I know that isn't a nice thing to think, but I guess I was still bitter about the day they pushed me. I told Looney that Rob beats and controls Nelly, and then his attention turned to Slim; the rest is self-explanatory. That is why Slim ran away.

Looney's facial expression and complexion changed. I could see he was fighting back tears. He stood there in silence for a few minutes, knowing if a word came out, so would a windfall of tears. He quietly walked in the house.

Kat and I waited. I saw the excitement in Kat's eyes, and I was trying my hardest not to jump up with joy. Looney came out and demanded we show him who Rob was. He didn't even speak to his goons. I told Looney that Rob worked during the day. I also reminded Looney that Slim didn't like violence and she loved her mom too much to even retaliate against Rob.

Looney started swinging his arms and swearing and stating he didn't give a fuck. I quickly interrupted and told him I agreed with him. "Heck," I said, "I can't stand Rob, but you just have to do things right. Think about Slim and the baby--they will need you. I am not telling you not to hurt Rob; I want to hurt Rob too. But I am letting you know, Slim won't want to be with you if she finds out."

Kat quickly interrupted and said that Rob came home by 6:15 p.m. "He takes the D train on Newkirk to and from work. Meet us at the pizza store by the train station by 5:50 p.m., and we'll show you Rob. Rob leaves early and comes home late. You decide when it's the best time to get him and how."

Kat and I left after Looney agreed on a time and went to King Plaza Mall. We got bored and then went to Prospect Park. We didn't want to go home or link up with anyone. We just wanted to kill time and not miss our appointment with Looney.

We made it to the pizzeria by 5:40 p.m. Looney was already there. We ordered food, ate it, and kept an eye out for Rob. Kat spotted Rob first. We pointed him out and Looney's face lit up. Kat and I stayed in the pizzeria to finish eating our food. Surprisingly, Looney had come alone, and he stayed with us to finish eating. He asked about Slim again. Looney wanted to know if Slim had asked about him or if she was coming to visit him. The truth was, Slim did ask about Looney, even though I didn't want to hear it.

I told Looney yes, she did, but we were not allowed to travel alone because of Rob. He looked frustrated. I told him I would come to Rodgers Avenue with her soon. Kat bumped my knee underneath the table because I guess she wasn't falling for the love act. I felt bad because I think he really cared for Slim. After eating, Kat and I ordered a beef patty and cocoa bread for Slim. That was her favorite. We left so Rob wouldn't see us.

When I got to the apartment, Slim was watching television. I gave her the beef patty and cocoa bread as a mini bribe. I felt bad for leaving her in the house, but sometimes you have to do things for the greater good. Slim asked me where I had been, and I made up some story about meeting up with an ex from school. She wasn't pushy because she still felt bad about everything and she thought Kat was still mad at her.

We all knew it wasn't her fault. We were upset about the situation, but not at her. I didn't blame her, I felt sorry for her. We watched movies until we both fell asleep on the couch.

THE PLAN

A couple of days went by and nothing happened. Kat and I began to think that Looney was all talk and no action. It was around 8:30 p.m., and we heard banging at the door. I ran to go check on who was knocking on the door, but Amelia stopped me. I heard screaming and it was coming from Rob.

My mom told Slim to go stay in the room with the twins. She grabbed the wooden bat that she kept in the coat closet and told me to grab the machete between her mattresses. Amelia made three calls that night. She then got on the telephone to call 911 and then she made another call to someone else. I didn't know who. She was whispering. I heard her say in Creole it had to be done tonight. Then she called Dalia and told her what was going on.

Amelia screamed through the door that Rob should leave because the cops were on their way. He said he wanted them to come. Rob kept rambling something about getting jumped or something. Amelia didn't make the situation better because she said, with a sarcastic tone, "So that's where the blood is coming from."

That comment only further enraged Rob. I, on the other hand, felt awful about what was going on. It was my fault. I didn't expect this mess to come to my door. I obviously hadn't thought it all the way through.

I prayed that the cops would come quickly because Amelia was not playing with Rob. I didn't want my mother to go to jail for this sick pervert; he wasn't worth it.

However, at the same time, I was happy to see Rob hurt, and his clothes soaked with blood. The hallway was drenched with blood. The police officers arrived to a messy scene. Rob was still cursing every single profanity there was in the English language. There were four officers that came to the scene.

Amelia quickly opened the door. Officers Rodriguez and Simon approached my mother. Officer McNeil and the other officer approached Rob. Looking back, they created a human barrier between Rob and Amelia. Officer McNeil asked Rob what the problem was and if he had a place to stay.

The police officers assumed it was a domestic violence issue. They asked him how he got hurt, and he quickly began to ramble about how "this crazy Haitian bitch got me jumped." They then turned their attention to Amelia.

Amelia stayed calm. She stated that the pervert lived down the hall. "I don't know how he got hurt and I do not appreciate him knocking at my door. His stepdaughter is living here." Rob started screaming, "This crazy bitch got me jumped," as if he hadn't said it before.

Rob wanted my mother arrested, as if she were the criminal instead of him. Amelia responded that she didn't know what he was talking about, but the children in this building were not safe in this neighborhood.

Slim stood there with tears on her face. I hadn't noticed her coming out of the apartment. Officer McNeil asked, "Who is this young lady?" pointing at Slim. Amelia told him that Slim was Rob's stepdaughter.

Amelia told Officer McNeil that she filed a complaint against Rob. He asked Slim if she wanted to talk about anything, and asked Amelia if he could come into her apartment to speak with Slim. Amelia asked Slim if that was okay with her, and she nodded yes.

By this time, all the neighbors had come of out of their apartments to see what was going on. Kat was there, and we exchanged a quick smile because we knew how Rob had gotten hurt and we were about to have him out of our lives for good. Amelia went into the house, which puzzled everyone. When she came out, she smiled at Rob, and then took a piece of white cloth she was carrying and wiped off a spot of Rob's blood that stained the wall next to our door.

Amelia said, "I'm crazy Rob, the fate you wish for is the fate you will get." Rob's mouth dropped and it appeared that he lost all his courage. He was not afraid of the police officer or the fact that Slim was talking about how he raped her, but he was afraid of Amelia's statement as she wiped his blood off the wall.

People are afraid of the unknown and he didn't know what was coming to him. The worst part was he did it to himself. He had the tool and he picked his destination by his words. Little did Rob know that his fate was sealed the minute he touched Slim. God looks after the fatherless and everything that is done in the dark shall come to light. Rob looked dazed.

The officer told him he needed a place to stay and that he couldn't stay in this building. The officer's words seemed to comfort Rob. Rob assured Officer Simmons that he would be leaving the building. He disclosed that he would be leaving the borough. We wouldn't ever have to worry about seeing him again. Nelly was not worth all this trouble.

As he turned away, he noticed that all of Amelia's sisters were standing there, like Spartan warriors ready to attack. Their small stature, beauty, and elegance could not hide their hatred and willingness to attack Rob. They had the cold, silent stares of Japanese samurai, quiet and deadly. Rob knew he had bitten off more than he could chew. I felt a cold chill in the hallway that summer night.

Rob noticed all of the first-floor neighbors standing outside their doors. Everyone was out except for Nelly. She was hiding. I don't know if it was out of fear or shame, or maybe Rob beat her up again. Families stood there with cold stares at him. He was exposed as a pervert, coward, and a poor excuse for a man.

As he passed my aunts, he politely said "Excuse me." After passing by, he noticed Stanley William with his arms crossed. Stan was an ex-boxer who fell on hard times after killing an opponent in the ring. His opponent had a heart condition, which he hid from the world. The guilt drove Stan to alcohol. To make matters worse, his wife left him shortly after giving birth to his twin daughters, Samantha, and Tabitha. They were older than us, but he guarded them like they were his prized possessions.

The twins looked just like their mother. Stan taught the neighborhood kids without fathers to box at the local YMCA and he was well respected in the community. As Rob passed by, Stan told Rob not to come back again. Stan had Rob by 50 pounds of muscle and three inches in height. Stan repeated his statement.

Rob nodded his head in silence, as it was understood what the consequences would be if he came back to Newkirk. By now Kat and I were standing next to each other and quickly sharing glances of satisfaction whenever things got worse for Rob. So much was going on that I couldn't contain myself.

I shouted, "Don't come back," with a voice broken up by tears. "Don't ever come to my door and try to hurt my family and friends." Amelia stood next to me and said, within Rob's hearing range, "I don't think he will have sense to find us." A teenage boy yelled out he would get hurt if he came back here.

Through all of this, I noticed that Nelly had not come out. I guessed she was looking out through her peep hole because she was ashamed. Everyone knew now. I fully understood the statement about "what is done in the dark will come to light." I was almost satisfied. Exposure is the best weapon.

Rob was about to walk away, but Officer McNeil came out with Slim standing right next to him. She looked like the little girl that she was. Although she had tears in her eyes, something was different. She no longer had the eyes of a scared, hurt, little girl. Her eyes belonged to someone who was determined and ready to fight. Rob knew what was coming next.

Officer McNeil grabbed Rob's wrist and put the cuffs on. He then read Rob his Miranda rights. The neighbors stood there, knowing that their suspicions were confirmed of what went on in that dimly lit, cigarette-filtered apartment.

Rob didn't even get a chance to leave the building as a free man. Everyone was clapping as Rob left in handcuffs. He was arrested and that saved his life. He really didn't know the fate that was waiting for him.

We were all happy he went to jail and had been

exposed. There was an investigation of his assault. Rob was seriously hurt. He had broken ribs, open wounds, and bruises. He disclosed it was not Amelia or any woman. There was an anonymous tip by a concerned citizen who described the assailant, which led the police to question Looney.

Looney denied any knowledge of the incident or even knowing Slim. Shortly afterwards, he moved out of state. A few months on Rikers Island made him reevaluate his decisions and lifestyle. Slim told Looney she had a miscarriage when he was at Rikers. She really had an abortion. This severed their ties and their relationship ended. He was grieving and decided that there was no reason for them to be together.

This was good news for Slim and Kat and me. Every obvious threat for now was gone; we had the rest of the summer and we were getting ready for high school. Kat and I slowed down with flirting and hanging around with different type of boys. We were pushed so hard that we realized how fragile we were and there were more than four types of boys. We realized we couldn't fit everyone into nice little boxes. People have layers like Amelia said. We slowed down and realized we still wanted to be young and be kids.

GROWTH

Allll of this seemed to have happened a lifetime ago. It's been six years. So many things have happened since then. Rob was incarcerated and was brutally raped in prison. The last I heard about him was that he went crazy. The name he called Amelia happened to him. Several young ladies came forward after he was arrested, and his picture made the newspaper.

Rob was a serial molester. He targeted children from single mothers with drug and alcohol issues. He targeted women who didn't have support or an active male in their life. He was a predator. He was a special type of evil.

Slim secretly had an abortion and never had the baby. She couldn't see herself having a baby by Rob. Very few people were aware of her pregnancy. She decided to move in with her grandmother, Mrs. Sharon Johnson, instead of moving in with my family. Mrs. Johnson lived on East 13th and Beverly Road. Slim fell in love with the neighborhood. It was quiet and beautiful.

That made Slim angrier that Nelly had grown up in such a nice block and gave her a dark apartment that reeked of cigarettes, alcohol, and depression. She didn't want to live close to Nelly. She wanted to forget. She had a chance to start new and she took it. Nelly had kept her children away from her family in order to hide her drug abuse and lifestyle. Her grandmother had no idea about what had happened until she read it in the paper.

Nelly had a normal upbringing with two hard-working parents. She had it better than most. But, she fell in love with the street life. Then she was trapped and never turned back. I think it was a combination of shame, drug use, depression, and the feeling of being trapped. I see why Nelly feared almost everyone. She wasn't raised in the hood; she was just a victim of it.

Slim went back to high school and graduated a semester early. She now had the home and family she always wanted and deserved. Kat and I would visit her sometimes. She looked very happy. She no longer looked like a sad puppy.

Slim looked beautiful. Her house looked like something from the Cosby Show or the Brady Bunch. Her old life seemed like a lifetime ago. Slim didn't even associate with anyone from the old neighborhood. I think we were her only close black friends. She had another black friend named Christie. Christie was Slim's best friend now. We met her other friends.

Slim was attending Brooklyn College and planned on becoming a doctor. She brought up Looney one time. She told us Looney was arrested in Georgia. He was linked to a string of robberies. He received the maximum sentence in federal prison. He didn't change. Her mother mailed her a letter Looney sent to Slim using her old Newkirk address. I think she thought she was doing Slim a favor.

Slim was upset about the letter because she never wanted to hear from him. She wanted to forget the past. I didn't blame her. I think the only reason she mentioned it to us was because we were the only ones that would understand. Her past did not fit with her new life and the life she planned for herself.

The newspaper never disclosed Kat's name because she was a minor. It was by luck that her grandmother figured out the article was about her. Kat and I never told her how we helped her get rid of Looney and Rob. We just sped up the process a bit. We never told anyone. We were fortunate it didn't blow up in our faces. No one ever knew we were the good, concerned citizens that described the mugger who had attacked Rob. We never shared that we knew Looney.

Slim was upset because she was engaged and planning a wedding to the man of her dreams. Slim felt like Nelly was sabotaging her. She swore she would never be like Nelly or date anyone that reminded her of Nelly's type. She didn't want a reminder of what happened to her under Nelly's care.

Slim was engaged to a fireman name Connor. He was madly in love with her. They were in love with each other. He was Irish and came from three generations of firemen. His family was nice but got wild when they drank. They welcomed Slim and respected her grandparents. Slim chose her best friend, Christie, to be her Maid of Honor.

Kat and I were to be bridesmaids, as well as Connor's three sisters and one of Slim's cousins. Connor sister's names were Chloe, Emma, and Meagan. They were very close but were always fighting. Slim met Christie when she moved in with her grandmother. They were the only two children on the block. Christie 's mother used to be Nelly's best friend. She died of a crack overdose.

Christie and Slim had so many things in common. They were both being raised by their grandparents. Slim and Christie had hard childhoods until their grandparents stepped in and rescued them.

I was secretly happy that Slim had moved in with her grandmother. I still felt betrayed because of the information they knew about my grandfather. I had so many things I needed to figure out about my family, and I needed my privacy at that time.

I didn't want to share that experience. I didn't really want to share Amelia, the twins, Aunt Nene and Tracey. I cherished my family despite their flaws or their pasts. Slim was also the only child at her grandmother's house. Her grandmother is a retired nurse and treats her very well.

Slim was happy that her family consisted of more than a drug-addicted mother who treated her poorly. Her aunts, uncle and cousins loved her, and she described them as normal. Slim, Kat and I were all still close, but we went through different high schools.

Kat and I still lived across the hall from each other. We had nightmares and felt awkward passing by Nelly's apartment. Nelly never moved away. She had no shame. We had a visual reminder of what happened. Kat and I continued to share secrets and think of ways to get out of awkward situations despite going to different high schools. Being in different high schools helped us grow as individuals. I participated in several school activities and met new friends.

Kat met many new friends as well. Sometimes our new friends would hang out with us. We never really liked each other's friends. I guess our new friends didn't reflect who we were, or maybe we were just jealous of each other's new friends.

Kat attended John Jay College of Criminal Justice and wanted to become a lawyer. That is a career choice that fits her personality. She was always strong-willed and focused, and she pays attention to detail. She is charismatic. Kat can get people to do things for her and make them feel like it was their idea or that she deserved more. She was also valedictorian of her high school. She is very ambitious; she works hard and parties harder than me. She was my best friend.

My partner in crime. Kat was dating this law student named Ryan. He was equally ambitious. He worked as a civil service employee for the city of New York. He works at the courthouse. He was accepted to do a summer internship years ago and they loved his work ethic and kept him. He was intelligent, handsome, and very ambitious.

Ryan was 5 foot 10 inches tall, small built, with dark skin. He was six years older than Kat. He wore a low fade haircut, was clean cut, and carried a brush to keep his wave in place. I was happy for Kat. They travelled a lot together.

Ryan was a single dad of a six-year-old boy. His son was named "R.J.," short for Ryan Jr. Ryan's mother helped him raise his son. Ryan didn't always have it together. He was a momma's boy. Fatherhood helped whip him into shape.

The mother of his child was not willing to sacrifice her life and future for an immature boy, so she dropped R.J. off and told Ryan she was leaving. Her exact words were: "Let you and your momma raise him since she wants to do everything." She was accepted to attend Florida State. She got on the plane and never came back, not even for summer breaks.

Ryan's hands were tied. Kat fell in love with Ryan and R.J., who looked just like his father. Kat was secretly happy about R.J., because she didn't want any kids until her late twenties or early thirties. She liked the fact that they were an instant family.

Ryan's mother had learned her lesson about trying to control his relationships. She had no choice but to help take care of her grandson. His mother loved Kat. She secretly told me that Ryan's ex-girlfriend never wanted a child and wanted to leave. She realized Kat was not a pushover. She met Kat's mother and realized Kat had a backup. Kat and Ryan were also engaged, although a wedding date hadn't yet been set.

I, on the other hand, attend college and I, too, party hard. I have a softer side because of the ordeal I went through. I have trust issues because of what I've seen and what I've experienced. Of my friends, I am the only one who is single and I'm happy about it. I look at things differently than people and other ladies my age.

I decided that I wanted to be a doctor. I decided to go to St John's University in Staten Island. I picked the Staten Island campus because it was smaller and more laid back. The Queen's campus was crowded, and it felt like high school to me.

I wanted a different feel and atmosphere so I could better focus. I was paying for this education, or at least my mother was. I wanted to leave Brooklyn for at least two days of the week. I made sure I fit all my classes into two days. My first semester was good; I had a GPA of 3.8.

The first day of the second semester felt like any other day. I tried to stay beneath the radar. I wore light gray Nautica sweatpants, a light gray Gap t-shirt, and a navy blue and grey pair of Nike air max. My hair was pulled back in a ponytail. I was early for class because I liked to sit in the back of the class closer to the exit. I liked seeing everything that went on.

My first class was history. I personally love history because it's something you cannot change. It was always an easy "A." This class was even better because the professor had a sense of humor. The professor was an older Irishman name Mike Kelly. He added humor and made fun of his family which kept us laughing.

This tall, goofy kid walked in late while we were laughing. He was about 6 foot 5 inches and had a mocha brown complexion. He wore a fade haircut and I can still see his wave. He had sleepy eyes and freakishly long eyelashes for a boy. He had full juicy lips and very high cheekbones. I could tell he looked like his mother because of his soft, feminine features. He had a gentle, exotic face. He had on navy blue Nautica sweats, a Nike t-shirt, and carried a basketball in his hand. The only empty seat was next to me.

As he walked to sit next to me, he was greeted by several male and female students. The professor even greeted him by his first name. I was just mad he took my book bag seat.

Professor Kelly started asking questions about the lesson he had just gone over and to my surprise Goofy raised his hand and knew the answers. He had a southern accent and was very polite with his answers. He was even polite when he debated with the other students on his point of view. He was really into the lesson.

He actually smelt good, and he wore cool water cologne. I admit his cologne caught my attention, but that was about it. I decided a long time ago never to talk to someone that went to the same school as me. I needed the freedom to walk away. Why was I thinking about this man? The bell rang, thank God. I walked at a good pace to make it to the next class.

The second class was psychology. This goofy kid was there first. I found out his name was Steven. He was sitting in the back of the class surrounded by a three-crew groupie. I sat in the corner in the back of the class by the window. I overheard that Steven was on the basketball team and he was from Georgia.

Steven also participated in this class. He was smart but not a pushover. He was country nice. He smiled and kept a nice tone as he embarrassed other students who challenged his intelligence. The polo wearing type who were told they were brilliant all of their lives. The kind of man that used their intellect to bully others. This time they picked the wrong one. This was actually a class I had been looking forward to take. It's abnormal psychology.

I had a long day ahead; I take six classes for two days a week. I prefer having five days to myself. This semester felt different somehow. The bell rang and Steven said hi and winked at me. His three-groupie bodyguards looked upset but didn't say anything because they knew better.

I'm quiet, but nothing about me appears timid or scared. I had more important things to do like eat and then buy my books. I only had an hour break until the next class. I rushed to the cafeteria to buy a muffin and tea for brunch. The cashier line in the cafeteria was extremely long, but I knew what I wanted to get and where everything was. I paid for it and rushed to the bookstore.

The line there was also extremely long, and I didn't think I'd have enough time to buy my books. I was just going to have to look for it and have the student bookstore workers hold it for me. I'd pay for it during my next break or make a trip back tomorrow to buy it. I found a worker and was giving them my name when I heard someone called out "Empress." I looked to see who it was, and it was Steven.

Steven was the third person in line. I was happy and confused at the same time. I walked over to him and he immediately said that he had been waiting for me and it had taken me long enough. He wasn't able to hold my spot any longer. I was amazed by his quick thinking and I played along.

I offered him some of my muffin, but it didn't sound right which made me feel embarrassed. I told him lunch was on me. He deserved it and I meant it. I paid for my book and put it in my pink Jansport book bag. I waited for him so I could pay for his lunch. That was the least I could do. He walked me to my next class, and I was surprised he was not in it.

I noticed both male and female students were staring at us as we walked down the hall. Last semester people tried to date me, and I never let them get close. Steven was new to St. John's University and already had a fan club.

I found myself daydreaming and hoped to see him through the course of the day. I kept expecting him to walk into the class late or find him sitting there already. I felt like I did in junior high school with Keith. I really hadn't had a crush on anyone since Keith.

My last class was math. I can't stand math. I walked

in and had an automatic smile. Steven was there and he had a seat saved for me. He greeted me in French. He said, "Bonjour Madame." I responded with "Bonjour Monsieur," and gave him a puzzled look, like how did he know. This man was full of surprises. He told me that some of his family was Geechy. I personally didn't know what that meant but I smiled anyway. I didn't have time for small talk because the professor jumped right into teaching.

The first few problems were easy, but then it got very complicated. Steven was raising his hand and shining like usual. I didn't expect him to be like this from first glance. I thought he was some dumb goofy jock. The bell rang and I was happy to run out of that math class.

Steven asked me where my next class was. I answered that he should already know because he seemed to be in most of my classes. Steven just laughed and said yes, he was stalking me.

Steven was a combination of both Keith and James. He was a smart athlete and had the attributes of my dream man. Steven and I started eating lunch together. We discussed our class work and families.

One day we decided to leave the campus for lunch. He was so excited to leave the campus. I was shocked, but I acted like I didn't notice his enthusiasm. We drove to LaBon Bonnaire Restaurant. I ordered a cheeseburger with fries and he ordered a breakfast platter.

Steven kept staring at me while I was eating. He was happy because usually girls our age never finished their meal. We dove into a deeper conversation. Steven told me that he was from Georgia. He had an older brother named

Damian. He was raised by a stern uncle. His mother had died of a broken heart because his father left and was never heard from again.

Steven looked like he wanted to cry when he was talking about his parents, especially when he talked about his mother. He really didn't care much for his father. He felt that his father was the reason the family suffered.

His father had gone to NYC and never looked back. His grandparents helped out the best they could, but it was not their responsibility. Steven's mother received a letter that his father had gotten married and started a new family. That's when their mother died. There were plenty of rumors. His mother just stopped doing everything. She stopped eating or talking or taking care of them.

Steven's family found him in a diaper full of dry feces. His brother was living off peanut butter. His mother just laid there without responding to anyone. She was committed to a mental hospital where she eventually died two weeks later. People say she died of a broken heart. He was too young to remember but was told this by distant family members and people from his town.

His Uncle Nelson was strict and reserved. His uncle had a temper and blamed the world for his problems. The neighborhood kids picked on Steven and his brother until they were big enough to defend themselves.

That was one of the saddest childhood experiences I had ever heard. I felt so bad for Steven. I realized how fortunate I had been. I asked him why he came to NYC, and he said he received a full scholarship and wanted to start anew. He had no real attachment to where he grew up, and he thought he was a burden to his Uncle Nelson.

Steven's uncle wasn't very kind to him or anyone. Steven felt like he and his brother were a burden to him and his family. He never felt included or like a part of the family. His Uncle Nelson didn't make life easy for them or make an effort to make them feel comfortable at his home. He didn't do anything special for them.

Steven and his brother joined sport teams and after school programs to limit their interaction with their uncle. Sports made them happy. Their uncle was never physically abusive toward them. Steven joined the softball and basketball teams while his brother Damian ran track and played football.

Steven felt like his uncle sabotaged him. He barely wanted to sign their permission slips. He would stare at the permission slip, make a face, take a deep sigh, and then signed it. It was always the same routine.

Steven and Damian would walk to practice by themselves. They would do odd jobs so they could buy their proper sports supplies. They would cut lawns in the summertime and weekends. They understood that their uncle couldn't afford their equipment.

Their Uncle Nelson only began showing interest in them when they started getting attention from the local newspaper and news channel. Steven and his brother's names started coming up in his workplace, his circle, and church.

His uncle Nelson began to ask them to bring their cousins to their games. He even wanted them to groom their cousins that he had spoiled over the years. Their Uncle Nelson's sudden interest was a shock. He wanted his children to play well in sports like him.

Steven found out that his uncle and father were best friend and teammates. The people in town compared Steven and Damian to his Uncle Nelson and his father. His uncle even started shooting hoops with them. The only thing his uncle Nelson had ever done with them was fishing. Steven hated it so much that he stopped eating fish.

Steven had decided at the age of 12-years old, that he was going to rely on himself. He realized that he was much taller than most kids his age, so he started to play basketball. He also spent most of his time alone, reading.

Steven didn't really like the kids in his town. They all heard about how his mother died and they weren't too kind. His older brother had it worse. He actually remembered everything and had fought a lot defending their mother. I asked him if anyone knew why his father left. He said no one knew for sure. I hugged him when he told me the story. I asked Steven why had he come to St. John's and he responded in a joking manner, "to meet you."

I thought Amelia would love Steven. She wanted me to stop dating dangerous people and limit my interactions with people who played with danger. At first, Amelia didn't like Steven, but she didn't press the issue. She said he had a familiar spirit. I ignored her and thought she was just being protective or Haitian.

Haitian mothers are very protective of their children. I loved my mom, but she didn't like anyone when it came to her children. I slowed down my clubbing because of Steven. We were seeing each other almost every day. We started dating after our first lunch at LaBon Bonnaire.

Things happened so fast. My house became his second home. He had no family in NYC. His brother promised to visit him but that hadn't happened. He was busy. He stayed in Georgia to play college football.

Steven was very protective of me and didn't want to bring me to Georgia. He didn't like the home he grew up in. He didn't like his uncle, aunt, or cousins. He didn't hate them, but he could live without them for a while. The only person he missed other than his brother was his Uncle Jerome.

Jerome was not his biological uncle. He was just someone that knew his father and looked out for him from time to time. He bought them Christmas gifts and school supplies. He had even sent them to camp one summer. He would go to their games.

Steven didn't feel like he belonged in Georgia with his uncle and his family. His uncle did not want him to come to NYC. Steven was upset about that. His Uncle Jerome supported his decision and had helped him select St. John's University.

Amelia thought we were moving too fast. I just thought she was being paranoid. I should continue to date thugs, ballers, rappers, and guys who liked fast cash and even faster women. I never dated drug dealers. I just didn't like the fact that they ruined families. It was a personal choice because of my Aunt Nene. I couldn't imagine being with someone who could help ruin lives like my Aunt Nene's. I knew I sounded like a hypocrite because of my dad, but I didn't know the man.

I could never like or fake-like someone who hurts people like that. I was a challenge to a thug, baller, or rapper. Being a virgin and not being from their world made me a challenge. I didn't need them financially so they couldn't buy me. I was not into drugs or alcohol and I'm not very materialistic. Some of them also knew about my dad and he was a legend in the streets of New York City. They kept trying to figure out my angle.

I was searching for love. I never told anyone that, but I wanted the love Amelia had with my dad without the heartache. There was no angle. I either felt love and safe or I didn't.

Steven was different from the guys I dated in the past. He was different from any of the guys our age. He was a star in the making. I think I purposely dated those guys because I didn't want to love anyone.

I didn't want real love to exist so I could avoid real pain. The pain of a broken heart that causes you to lay in bed, silent and confused. I wanted the magical love that's supposed to last forever.

Steven was funny, goofy, helpful, athletic, and smart. He opened up to me. He was sensitive. He was attached to me. There was no losing this one. He came around the house a lot to study and to eat Amelia's cooking. He helped me with my math assignments.

Steven even warmed up to the twins. The twins loved him, especially Prince. Prince was always the only American male around other than my cousin Reginald. Steven even showed Prince some of his basketball moves. Prince enjoyed having someone to play basketball with. Prince was getting very good at it too. He was bragging to his friend about playing basketball with Steven.

Steven gave Prince one of his jerseys before he gave

me one. I acted like I was jealous, but I was secretly happy. I barely had any alone time with Steven. Prince and I even went to some of his games.

Steven loved NYC. He said meeting me was the best thing that had happened to him. He stayed at my house so much that the people from the neighborhood started to know him. They saw him play, but they didn't know who he was. Once he wore his uniform to my house after games, the questions began. Everyone was interested in his games. He answered a couple of their questions and kept it moving.

Steven didn't really trust people because of how he was treated growing up. I was happy he was like that, and that he wasn't a crowd pleaser. I remembered one time when he went to the store, a kid named Lawrence approached him with small talk.

Lawrence was a shady character. He was considered shady in all circles. He had a love-hate relationship with me. He liked me, but hated that I didn't feel the same. Lawrence was a loner because no one trusted him. Lawrence was the only person in the neighborhood that tried to get young kids to sell drugs and rob the drug dealers from other neighborhoods.

No one wanted Lawrence around; even his own family couldn't stand him. They moved out of state just to get away from him.

Lawrence didn't have any friends his age. Lawrence had cut the conversation short when he saw me walking towards them. I asked Steven what he wanted. Steven said Lawrence had been talking about gambling and how he liked to win. Lawrence said he had heard that Steven was a college basketball star. Steven looked at me and said not to worry. "I didn't let it get to that point.

Lawrence was trying to flatter Steven so he could fix the game. Steven played country dumb. Steven knew Lawrence was not worth his scholarship or jail time. Anyway, I don't even know him, and I don't like him." I was so happy that he was able to read Lawrence and played country dumb.

This incident made me dislike Lawrence even more. He was a scavenger, a parasite. He should have never approached Steven. Steven was not part of the street.

I wanted Steven to meet Kat. Kat decided to bring Ryan along so she could get a feel of him but make it appear normal. I wanted my best friend to like Steven. I really didn't care about Ryan's opinion.

Ryan had his own faults. He was a recovering mama's boy. We drove to Staten Island to eat at Perkins. We went on a Wednesday, and the restaurant was quiet like we had hoped it would be. There weren't any familiar faces except for the waitress.

Steven and I would go there sometimes after his basketball games. He was excited to meet my friends. I could tell because he had on jeans. Steven usually wore sweatpants. He had on a pair of black Levi's jeans and a regular white t-shirt with a black and white Adidas symbol. He wasn't materialistic.

Ryan was used to being the only guy around us and was trying to test Steven's intelligence. He quickly realized that Steven was no dummy. I didn't make eye contact and even act like I knew what was going on. I was glad that Steven could handle himself with style. By the end of the evening, Ryan and Steven were acting like best friends. Ryan was asking Steven about his games and promised to come see him play.

Steven was asking Ryan about law school. Ryan asked Steven if he picked a major, to which Steven proudly replied that he was pre-med, like me. Steven told Ryan that we were in many of the same classes. I couldn't help but blush.

Kat blurted out "I like him. Anyone that can make my best friend blush is alright with me." Kat quickly looked at Ryan and said, "Don't worry baby, I love you." Kat quickly turn to Steven and asked when we could meet his people.

Steven quickly answered that his parents were dead, and he only had his uncle's family and a brother. There was an uncomfortable silence. Steven broke the ice by saying his brother might visit soon; however, the date wasn't set in stone. Kat replied that we couldn't wait to meet him.

Kat turned to me and said, "Speaking of meetings, we are supposed to meet next weekend to pick out the bridesmaid dresses." I quickly told Kat I'd forgotten about it, but she knew I was lying. She realized she messed up. I hadn't mentioned it to Steven because I wasn't sure I was going to bring him to Slim's wedding.

Ryan quickly added that he was going to attend. Ryan was making things worse for me because he wanted a "one up" on Steven. Steven didn't participate in this conversation nor did he act like it bothered him.

Kat quickly changed the conversation and playfully asked Steven if he loved her friend. Steven blushed and was acting goofy. We all started teasing him. The night was fun, and we planned on doing it again. We said goodbye and Kat whispered, "I'm sorry" in my ear and "I'll call you later."

Kat and I have our own language. We shared secrets that no one knew and would never leave our lips. Our bonds were stronger than any relationship we had with any man. We never knew when we might have to regroup and fix future problems. We learned to never show our hands, no matter how much we were in love. Kat left with Ryan. He drove a Chrysler that his mom bought for him

I picked Steven up in my black Nissan Maxima that my mom bought for me. That was my high school graduation gift. Amelia wanted me to be safe when I traveled to school. My mom acted like Staten Island was a different country. I knew she just wanted to give me a car but didn't want it to appear that she was spoiling me. The twins were watching and couldn't wait to graduate high school--they were expecting a car too.

The car ride back was quiet, and I broke the ice by asking Steven if he wanted to go back to the campus or do something else. He quickly answered that I was driving. So, I told him that we were going to Brooklyn and we were taking the long way there.

I drove the car to the ferry so we could sit and talk. This was the first time he had traveled on the Staten Island Ferry in a car. Since he was trapped, I asked him what was his problem. I already knew what was wrong with him. Of course, he said nothing. I asked Steven if it was about the wedding.

I told him Slim was a childhood friend of mine, and her wedding was not my first priority. I told him

I was too wrapped up with school, our relationship, his games, and family and that it had slipped my mind. I held Steven's hand and asked him if he would be my date for the wedding. I told him I didn't know how to ask him.

Steven's face immediately lit up. He gave me a passionate kiss, which caught me completely off guard. He started talking about renting a tuxedo. He had never worn a tuxedo before. I found out Steven hadn't gone to his high school prom. Despite being one of the most popular kids in his town, he stayed to himself and his immediate family.

Steven never forgave his town for teasing him about his mother's shame and death, and their mistreatment towards his family. I made a mental note to never cross Steven and to try to never hurt him. I laid my head on his shoulder for the rest of the ferry ride. We both remained quiet. I didn't want the night to end, so I asked him if he wanted to go to Coney Island by the beach or Atlantic City. I loved the beach at night.

We were too young to drink or gamble, but the beach is always nice to me. We decided to go to Coney Island because it was closer. Steven knew Amelia would start paging me after a certain time; Momma Bear doesn't play around when it came to her children.

I was getting tired, so I let Steven drive us to Coney Island. He needed directions, of course. He was playing "Around the Way Girl" by LL Cool J. He was looking at me like I was cake as he licked his lips like he was LL Cool J himself. He was lip-singing to me. I started popping my gum real hard as I swung my hair back and forth, as if I were in the video. We started laughing as soon as the song was done.

That's what I liked about Steven; we always clicked. We weren't dressed for the beach but that was okay. We walked along the board walk. I never realized how tall he was. We were holding hands and he looked down and said he loved me. I told him that I loved him too. That is why I loved the beach at night--there's something magical about it. I, personally, love the smell of the beach. I realized I liked it better at nighttime.

Steven held me and I felt so safe. I have never felt safe in a man's arms before in my life. I felt like it was just us. I started thinking about Amelia and Dad. This was probably how he made her feel. I remembered Amelia's speech when I was in junior high school, and realized she was right. Keith may have loved me, but he didn't show me love. We weren't ready. I'm not sure I'm even ready now. My pager went off and we quickly looked at each other and smiled. I thought it was Amelia, but it was Kat who paged me.

We walked to the nearest pay phone and I called her. She apologized again and I said everything was cool. I told her I was in Coney Island with Steven. That was a way to let her know I couldn't talk right now. I told her I'd meet up with her tomorrow. We only lived across the hall from each other. I used my last quarter to call Amelia afterwards. I told Amelia that I was in Coney Island with Steven and I was heading home.

My mom was always happy to hear from me. She knew about my meeting with Kat, Ryan, and Steven. We arrived in the neighborhood around 10:00 p.m. It took another hour to find parking in Brooklyn. Welcome to Brooklyn life.

The twins rushed to us once we got to the apartment. I loved them and, to my knowledge, Steven likes them. Amelia was there. She rushed the twins off to bed after they greeted us. Amelia offered us food. I was full but I knew Steven wanted some, so I said yes for the both of us.

Amelia told me to serve him and she did something else that surprised me. She said it was late, and if Steven wouldn't get in trouble, he could sleep in the guest bedroom. Steven's face lit up. She repeated with a stern voice, "In the guest bedroom." Steven said thank you and that he would stay in the guest bedroom.

The truth was, we were both virgins and wanted the first time to be special. We were not in any rush to lose our virginity. We both had trust issues and wanted real love. We had discussed being a virgin and how special the first time should be.

Amelia is strict, but she had a heart for other people's children. She didn't want him out there trying to get home alone or me out there trying to get him home. Amelia didn't want either one of us out in the streets. She began to have a soft spot for Steven once she found out he was an orphan. That day was one of the best days of my life. I had a date for the Slim's wedding.

Kat and my family loved Steven and he loved me. Everything appeared perfect. I am glad I stop clubbing and started spending more time with Steven. I slept peacefully knowing Steven was in the room next to me. I couldn't be in the same room with him. I was still grateful he was part of the family already.

I woke up the next morning thinking it was a dream, but then I heard my mom making breakfast and speaking to Steven. I quickly called Kat's telephone number to update her about last night. She was shocked that Amelia had permitted Steven to spend the night, even if he was in a different room. I told her that he was coming with me to Slim's wedding.

Kat was happy because she thought she created tension between Steven and I. I jokingly told her it was Ryan's fault. She was happy that I met someone that I loved. I was happy I met someone I loved too.

Kat was genuinely happy for me. She wanted us to be happy, married, successful and wealthy. We always talked about how we wanted our lives to be. We fantasized about being as wealthy as the characters in Dynasty, but we didn't want their dramatic personal love life's. We discussed Slim's wedding colors which were mint green and gold. She wanted green because her fiancé's family is Irish.

I didn't like the colors because I thought I would look like a peppermint. I didn't tell Slim that because it's her wedding and it wasn't about me. Slim needed to be loved and accepted by her in laws.

Slim needed that security. I knew she would always need to feel secure, more than the normal girl. I don't blame her. I asked Kat not to pick such ugly colors when it was her turn, and she asked me to not do the same. I told Kat I would speak to her later; I wanted to see what was going on in the kitchen.

I walked in the kitchen wearing my mini-mouse pajamas and my hair in high ponytail. I kissed and greeted

Amelia. Steven's face lit up when he saw me. He stood up and reached down to give me a half-sideway hug. The twins were eating their breakfast. They had to go to school soon.

Amelia cooked sausage, scrambled eggs, and grits with cheese. Steven was happy. He disclosed that he felt like he did when he was younger, living back home. This reminded him of the trips to his grandparent's house. He felt at peace in our apartment. The twins looked at everyone and stated they wanted to stay home. Amelia quickly replied that they needed to hurry up and eat so they could go to school.

Amelia didn't play around when it came to education. Good grades and attendance were a must in this house. The twins sighed and Prince said, "at least we tried," They kissed Amelia and I goodbye and gave Steven a hug. Steven didn't know what to do with himself. He felt like part of the family.

My mom asked us what our plans were for the day. Neither one of us had class that day. We didn't work so we both said "studying" at the same time. Then Steven mentioned basketball practice later. Amelia said okay and went to get ready for work.

Amelia worked as a registered nurse at Kings County Hospital. She loved her job and they loved her. Amelia came home with flowers, candy, and cards on every birthday and holiday. She's been there for over 20 years and had been named as Employee of the Year several times. She worked in the Intensive Care Unit for newborns. It wasn't as easy as one might think.

There were so many drug-addicted babies and babies

born with HIV. There were also premature babies, and some being born with rare ailments or severe medical issues. My mom used to feel bad for them and showed them love while using universal precautions. She sometimes fought back tears as she told me stories from work. The stories were one major reason I had kept my virginity.

Steven loved hearing stories about my family. He was fascinated with my family and our culture. He was happy that they embraced him. Steven disclosed that it was the first time he felt included as part of a family since his grandparents died. He had to fight back tears. I decided I wanted to cook that day.

Steven was joking how I couldn't cook, and I needed to wait for Amelia to throw down food. I laughed as I headed to the kitchen. I got out an already-seasoned bag of chicken (we cleaned and seasoned our meat as soon as we bought it). I put some red beans on to boil, and that day I cooked stewed chicken, red beans, and rice. He liked the food so much that I decided to fix him a plate to go. It felt nice to playhouse with him.

We showered and dressed so we could go to Steven's basketball practice. We had on sweatpants and t-shirts. Steven left some clothes at my house because he was always there. He lifted me off the ground and gave me a passionate kiss before we left the apartment. Steven loved picking me up and I loved that even more. He made me feel safe and loved. I think I gave him something to love.

The drive to Staten Island was long. We were in traffic on the Brooklyn Queens Expressway. We didn't mind because it gave us more time to be alone and talk. I was soaking up all this quality time. I imagined the rest of my life with him. I didn't tell him of course.

We made it to his practice on time, and I dropped him off and then went looking for a parking space. I usually met him inside when he was running late. We had our routine down like we had been doing it forever. It had only actually been nine months. This was the longest relationship that either of us had. In fact, this was his first relationship.

I went inside of the gym and there were people watching the team practice. This was the norm. Staten Island can be boring, so I didn't blame them. The team is really good. I walked in and sat on the benches across from where the team was sitting. I had a better view and I didn't want to appear too clingy.

I always sat by myself but today was different. There was a group of girls that came and sat behind me. It was weird because the gym was huge, and they could have sat anywhere they wanted. I already know some bullshit was about to happen. I ignored them and continued to cheer for the whole team. They already know that I was here for Steven. It was a click of three girls.

One of them was named Amanda. She was in one of my classes last semester. She was from California. She even knew how to surf. She was the first black girl that I knew of that could do that. She was mulatto.

Amanda made sure everyone knew that she was black, although she looked more like her father's Italian side of the family. Amanda had a pale complexion with dark colored hair. She had full lips and wide hips. She was about 5 foot 9 inches tall, and had an aggressive, fierce demeanor. She was very outspoken and appeared to know what she wanted.

Then there was Lynn, who was Korean. Her family owned a chain of Korean spas. Lynn always wore designer clothes, drove a BMW, and was into the hip-hop culture. Lynn was very petite, but also demanding. She acted like she was entitled. She was very smart, and she loved to party with rappers and reggae artists. She had a wild side. She usually had a backstage pass to popular rap, R and B and pop concerts.

Lynn gained a lot of attention due to her sleek wardrobe. I admit she did look nice and her diamonds were real. She always acted like she couldn't be bothered and had a short fuse. Lynn knew not to mess with me. She had tried once, and I embarrassed her. Lynn looked like she wanted to just disappear that day. I felt Kat in me.

Cindy was also part of this click. She was the cliché blond cheerleader. She was a cheerleader at St. John's University. Cindy had been a cheerleader most of her life and she's from Staten Island.

Cindy was an average Staten Island girl. She had a tan, high hair, and a face full of makeup. She was about 5 foot 9 inches. When they walked, Lynn was always in the middle of the runway girls. Amanda and Cindy earned that nickname because they were very tall and wore shoes, sandals, and boots with heals. They acted alike and were always together.

They tried to recruit me to be a part of their click three semesters back. I wasn't interested. I didn't like clicks. It's too much work and sometimes people are not genuine in a crowd.

I think they realized I had a no-nonsense attitude and wanted me to be a part of their mean-girl crew. I already had my own friends that I had found myself a long time ago. I heard Cindy ask the others which team member they thought was cute. I already knew this game. The same deviant games had been played before, but with a different group of girls. Lynn quickly answered Brian.

Brian was the closest thing to a best friend for Steven. Lynn described how he was always trying to get with her, and they started talking. I already knew that. Then Amanda said she thought Steven was cute.

I acted like I didn't hear her. Amanda started talking about how she made out with Steven last night. I quickly realized that was a lie. I was happy inside. I didn't react because Steven had spent the night at my house. I was thinking she sounded desperate. I listened to them talk. I was happy. Steven walked towards me after practice.

Amanda yelled and waved to Steven. He waved back to her and kissed me on the lips. I asked him if he liked my mom's Haitian cooking last night. He replied, "I always love her cooking, especially what she cooked last night." He hugged me and practically carried me off the bench. When I faced Amanda, I smiled and winked. I know Amanda felt dumb. I was just happy he was with me all day yesterday. I didn't want my heart broken again.

Steven and I headed to his dorm room. He quickly asked me what was that all about. I asked him what he was talking about. He said, "Asking about your mom's cooking." I laughed and said, "Amanda was telling me you were with her last night. She acted like she was talking to her friends. I knew you were with me and I wanted her to know you were with me." Steven laughed and said he had figured something was up and that's why he playfully carried me off.

Steven said he couldn't have them hurting his Haitian princess. I smiled and hugged him. I didn't even know where that came from as I'm not usually that mushy. Steven decided to change his clothes. He didn't go inside the bathroom like he usually did.

Steven was slim but full of muscles. He had and 8-pack abb. You couldn't tell by just looking at him. He just looked like an ordinary, slim 19-year old. Thinking about it, there was nothing ordinary about him. He was attending St. John's on a sports scholarship but was offered a science scholarship. He maintained a 4.0 grade point average. He was a smart athlete whose name appears in the newspapers all the time. He was one of the top college basketball scorers. He didn't act like he was a star, but he was.

Steven was just a kid trying to secure a good life. He gave me a hug and kiss while saying how much he would miss me. I told him that I missed him too. I watched him wave to me as I honked my horn. I loved the way he loved me. I imagined my future with him. He loved me and my family, and I couldn't wait to meet his family.

I arrived home and Amelia thanked me for cooking. Prince started poking fun at me. Prince said, "She didn't cook this." I laughed as I made myself a plate to eat. It had been an interesting day and I couldn't wait to speak to Kat about it, but then I looked at Amelia's face full of love and happiness. I realized I wouldn't have been so happy if she hadn't let Steven spend the night. I probably would have believed Amanda's lies.

I gave Amelia a huge kiss and hug and told her she was the best mom ever. Amelia looked surprised and concerned at the same time. She asked why. I told Amelia what happened in the gym and she was relieved. I kissed her on the cheek and whispered to Amelia, "Don't worry, we are both virgins." Amelia smiled and said, "That's good." I reminded her of and thanked her for the talk we had in junior high school. I decided certain things I should just keep to myself and family.

I showered and went to bed because I had to meet up with Slim and the bridal party the next day. I called Kat and asked her if she wanted me to drive or if she wanted to drive to Slim's house. Kat wanted to drive. I was glad because when it was time to leave, Kat would leave.

I set my alarm to wake me up at 11:00 a.m. I really didn't like waking up early on a Saturday morning. Tomorrow was the day to pick out bridesmaid dresses. We were supposed to meet at Slim's house for brunch and dinner. We would pick out our dresses sometime between then.

Slim was having a seamstress come over at 2:00 p.m., to show us her designs and measure us. We would alter our dresses just a little to fit our body type and personality. Her grandparents were paying for everything, including the dresses for the bridal party. Slim's grandparents were so proud of her that they would do anything to make her happy.

Slim was their second chance at parenthood. They blamed themselves for Nelly's life and wanted to do it right with Slim. They admitted how much they loved Nelly but not her life choices. I felt like it was going to be a long day. I decided to beep Steven to remind him of my plans.

Steven called me back immediately. He wanted to know if I was going to be able to make it to his game tonight. I told him I wouldn't miss it for the world. I had almost forgotten all about his game. We made small talk and I got off the telephone to go and get ready to leave. I headed to the bathroom to brush my teeth and shower.

Amelia went to work, and the twins were still sleeping. I made a big breakfast for us and I asked the twins if they wanted to come with me to Slim's house. Prince felt like it would be boring but would come with me later to see Steven play. Princess wanted to come. I told her she could help me pick out my dress. Princess was so excited.

Amelia and the twins were invited to the wedding. Slim was grateful to Amelia. Slim's grandparents had kept in contact with Amelia. I told Princess to pack some snacks for us just in case we got hungry.

Slim's grandmother loved the twins so I know she wouldn't mind Princess coming. I didn't mind her coming--maybe I was being selfish, but I wanted my baby sister to come. I wanted Princess to participate in this special occasion.

Princess was 13-years old and this was the best time to bond. We decided to dress alike. We were doing the twin thing. Princess loved dressing like me, and I thought it was cute since we looked alike. We had on red t-shirts, red and white air max sneakers, and black Levi's jeans. I put her hair in a high "I Dream of Jeannie" ponytail and

I let Princess do my hair the same way. I let her use my Estee Lauder lip gloss.

Princess was excited because she wanted to see what the gowns were going to look like, as well as the wedding dress. She wanted to feel like a part of it.

I knocked on Kat's door to pick her up. Surprisingly, Kat was ready. She looked relaxed with her side ponytail, white t-shirt, blue jeans, and blue vans. We hopped in Kat's car, although we could have easily walked to Slim's house. Slim's block had plenty of parking.

We arrived at her house around 12:30 p.m. Christie, Chloe, Emma, Meagan, and Slim's cousin, Renee, were already there. Kat, Princess, and I sat in the living room and talked to whoever was in there at the time. I didn't feel like cooking or stepping on anyone's toes. I made the decision not to get too involved in the planning. I was going to be a supportive friend and pick a dress style that fit my shape.

Christie and the Connor sisters were fighting for control of the wedding planning. I wanted no part of that. Christie had been fighting for years to be number one in Slim's life, and she was not going to give it up that easy. It was pretty sad. Christie felt like she was losing her best friend.

The Connor sisters had each other and really needed to let Christie plan her best friend's wedding. Christie was trying to hide her pain, but she looked like she was ready to cry. They should've let Christie have this. Slim didn't even back up Christie, as Christie looked at her for help.

The oldest of the three Connor sisters was Meagan. She was about 5 foot 7 inches and was slim built. She had blond hair and was very pale with grey eyes. She was a stay-at-home mom. She had worked at a bakery but stopped working because of her husband. He was a police officer and didn't want her working until their children were school age. She baked for family functions now.

Meagan had baked a carrot cake for today. The carrot cake looked like it had been purchased from a bakery. She bragged about the arrangement she had with her husband. She would cut coupons to secretly save money from what her husband gave her so she could open her own bakery. She had run the neighborhood bakery for years. She was helping Christie and Slim with the cake and menu for the wedding.

Meagan thought she was an expert. This wedding was important to her because of her brother and her ego. Meagan wanted to bake cakes and create lasting memories for people at special events. She wasn't going to let this opportunity pass by without putting her signature on it. Meagan had a small clientele. She baked for people around her neighborhood for a fee; her prices were good, and her baking was delicious.

Emma was the second oldest. Emma was about 5 foot 9 inches and looked like a model. She had jet black hair, full lips, pale skin, and grey eyes. She was the family saint. She graduated with a degree in accounting from Brooklyn College. She still lived at home and worked for Morgan Stanley during the week. She did the accounting for their family bar, The Lucky Leprechaun. She even helped out at the bar sometimes.

Emma was wild and crazy at the bar, but pretty toned down at work. Slim had met Connor at the bar. She had been coming from work wearing her scrubs when her car broke down. She walked into The Lucky Leprechaun to use the telephone to call for help. Connor had offered her help and they had been dating since then. Emma is single and beautiful.

Chloe was the youngest of the sisters. She was about 5 foot 5 inches tall, with red hair and green eyes. She also lived at home and worked full time at The Lucky Leprechaun. She was enrolled part time at the Kingsborough Community College. She was still finding herself; she followed no rules. She drank with her dad and brothers, and she would fight with anyone. No one really challenged her because of her brothers. She was just free spirited. When all of them got together, it was total chaos.

I was glad when lunch was ready. They made eggplant parmesan and Caesar salad. It was good. I usually didn't complain about a free meal. I found out the sisters had shopped for the food today. I just hoped there was meat with the dinner later. I was happy when I found out Slim's grandmother cooked dinner by herself because we had been busy.

Kat and I made eye contact and smiled. I couldn't wait for the seamstress to arrive because I was tired of the sisters fighting with each other and trying to bully Christie. Slim didn't say anything. They were nice to us, but we stayed quiet and they were trying to feel us out. We decided not to get too familiar with them because then they would treat us like they did each other.

They also cursed like sailors and drank like fish. Although it was funny, I held in my laughter. Princess would laugh and then they would apologize because they realized she's just a kid. They acted embarrassed and I acted like I believed them. That was their normal behavior.

Slim was walking on eggshells and didn't appear very happy. While Christie was not the nicest person, she didn't deserve that treatment from the sisters. They treated each other like that, so maybe it was a sign of love for Christie.

The seamstress arrived at 2:00 p.m. I expected someone old, but the seamstress was a tall, slim, Asian lady named Erica. She was in her early 30s. She wore earth-tone colors and natural stones in all her jewelry. Her aura was peaceful. Her expression, tone, and presence were relaxing. I didn't know where Christie found her, but I liked her already.

Erica had an artist's portfolio and her seamstress bag that contained her tools. She was making Slim's dress as well as dresses for the bridal party. Slim looked at the pictures of wedding dresses she had. She liked them, but she wanted her dress to be a little different. She wanted to add a little flavor. Slim was leaning toward a dress she had seen in Vogue magazine. I was getting excited about it.

Erica had samples of materials for our bridesmaid dresses. She had us feel the 2-inch x 3-inch samples of material. She had satin, sateen, charmeuse, crepe, and many more. We chose charmeuse. I started to envision myself in a mint green and silver gown. They all felt so nice that it was hard for us to choose the material in the beginning.

Erica measured us and took full control of the situation. I was surprised that the sisters were not bickering or getting on everyone's nerves. I was excited about the style I picked. My dress was going to be an "A" line /Princess V-neck, floor length. Kat wanted her dress to be strapless. All of our dresses had a split on the left side. We were all satisfied.

Erica's ideas pleased everyone. She made me see Slim's and Christie's visions; Erica brought their visions to life. The colors weren't that bad. The sisters had been drinking wine throughout the day. Erica took everyone's contact information. We could go to her business on our own time to pick up our dresses. Erica gave everyone her card and left.

We were all impressed by her professionalism. Slim was very happy and Christie was eating up the compliments. That was a victory for Christie. Christie then asked if everyone wanted just one hair stylist/cosmetologist to do everyone's hair and makeup. We all looked at each other for a second, and Meagan asked if they did white girl's hair.

We all burst out laughing, and Kat said, "You read my mind." Christie assured us that her girl could do all types of hair, and that it would be easier if they came to us and did everything. Chloe wanted to know how much it would cost. Christie said, "She's not expensive and we get a group rate." Christie went on about how her cousin used her and everyone looked nice and she's professional. Christie promised to come back with the price in a week. Christie knew everyone and had plenty of useful contacts.

Mrs. Johnson came to the living room to tell us dinner was ready. She told us to help ourselves because she was tired. I was so happy dinner was done because I had to leave soon. I wanted to be there for Steven. The kitchen smelled like Thanksgiving dinner had been cooked.

Mrs. Johnson was originally from South Carolina and can cook her some soul food. She cooked fried chicken, baked macaroni, collard greens, and sweet potato pie. She made fresh lemonade. I made a plate for Princess and myself. Kat fixed her own plate. The three of us ate in the living room while the others crowded into the kitchen.

They were drinking wine, being loud and making a mess. I saw why Mrs. Johnson took her plate and went to her room; she went to hide in her own house. I didn't blame her. Kat gave me the look that she was ready to leave. I was happy because I could take my plate to go. I liked Slim; I just didn't like Slim and company. I didn't like how Slim acted in front of her future in-laws. There were too many aggressive personalities together in one space. It felt uncomfortable to be there.

Kat and I went into the kitchen to say we were leaving. Chloe turned around and asked why and said it was early. We didn't even know we were liked or would be missed. Kat had been caught off guard, so I told them I was going to watch my boyfriend play basketball in Staten Island.

They were suddenly interested. Meagan asked "Where?" because they had cousins that lived in Staten Island. Slim answered for me and told them that my boyfriend was the star player at St. John's University. I was blushing.

Meagan asked, "Is it that McCoy kid?" with excitement. "Yes," I replied. "That's my Steven." Meagan asked if they could come and I said I didn't mind.

Meagan was so excited. She even knew that St. John's

was playing against Seaton Hall University. She knew more about the game than I did. I knew Slim was too wrapped up with her wedding, so I didn't invite her. I told the sisters I had to get my car and my little brother. I asked them if they wanted to follow me or meet me there. They decided they would meet me there. I was happy because that was less work for me.

Slim acted like she was excited about it. She hadn't shown genuine interest for months in what was happening in Kat's or my life. I knew deep down it was because she was getting the life, she never thought she could have. I knew she was trying to impress them. I knew my friend's heart. I loved her and she shouldn't try so hard. They would love her regardless.

I waved goodbye and they were so excited. I guess they weren't that bad. I asked Kat if she coming to Steven's game. She said she would come with me. I didn't want to be alone with the sisters just yet. I needed her to help me read them better. They were now coming into my world. Kat parked the car and we went to pick up Prince.

I kissed Amelia and told her my plans. She was happy. She loved it when I did things with the twins. The twins were excited. Prince was getting so tall and had grown to love basketball. Amelia liked that Steven took Prince under his wings. Amelia liked that Steven valued education. I asked my mom if she wanted to come, but she gave me a weak excuse about having to work in the morning. I told her how many people were coming with me and she was excited. Amelia thinks I should be open to meeting new people. I kissed Amelia goodbye and went to pick up Kat.

Kat and I discussed today's experiences. We were shocked that the sisters had wanted to tag along with us. We decided we should be open and give them a chance. Maybe we were nervous because Slim was nervous. Maybe we were feeding off her vibe. Slim was always scared and wanted to be liked by who she considered to be the right people.

Steven's game began at 8:00 p.m. We didn't get there until a quarter to eight, so I didn't get a chance to see Steven before the game. It was crowded as usual. Lucky for us, Slim, Christie and the sisters were already there and saved us seats. The seats were right behind the St. John's team.

Steven smiled and winked at me when he saw me. I smiled and stuck my tongue out at him. I noticed Amanda and her friends were sitting close to the team. They were one row in front of where Slim was sitting. Chloe waved at us to make sure we saw them. The sisters had been drinking all day.

I felt like the night was going to be interesting. I had already filled Kat in about Amanda and her amateur mean-girl crew. Kat was ready. They didn't know what they started. Kat was excited because she had been meaning to come to Steven's game. She called Ryan to meet us at St. John's. I felt good about this. The only person missing was Connor. He had to work. He always worked overtime.

Slim thought he was saving up for a house. He lived with two roommates who were also firemen. Amanda and her crew saw me, and their eyes followed me to where I sat down. They had the look of confusion and uncertainty on their faces. They never really saw me with other people. They must have assumed that my life revolved around school like theirs did. I actually had outside friends. I lived in the city all my life. I was not an out-of-state student.

They looked at each other and I didn't hear a word from them throughout the game. Once in a while they would look back, but they never spoke. They even tried to smile and join in when we booed the other team. I acted like I didn't know who they were and ignored them. Everyone felt my vibes towards them. I was not about to make nice with them, but I didn't want to be mean either.

Ryan arrived at the game 15 minutes late. He greeted everyone. He knew everyone except for the sisters. Kat had told Ryan they would be there, so he greeted them too. Prince was excited to see Ryan because he had been the only guy there. Everyone was excited, enjoying themselves. Our section cheered for Steven the loudest. I was happy that Steven had all this support from my circle. He was used to being cheered on by strangers and then go home to loneliness.

St. John's won the game; Steven was the top scorer, as usual. And, as usual, I was proud of him. We waited in the gym for Steven to change. He came out with Eric, Michael, and Brian. They were his teammates. Brian was the loud one in the group. He was a senior and was told by the coach to look after the new players.

Brian was from Staten Island. Brian's father was the basketball coach for St. Peters High School. Brian was practically born with a basketball in his hand. He knew the game and could play, but he most likely was going to be a coach or play for foreign teams. He wouldn't make it to the NBA, but he definitely received a free ride to college.

I introduced Steven and his friends to Slim, Christie, and the sisters. Steven introduced the twins and Ryan to his teammates. Brian of course noticed how much Princess looked like me.

Chloe was still bored, so she asked what we had planned for the rest of the night. The twin's faces lit up. I quickly said, "Not you guys."

Brian was excited because he loved women. That was probably the main reason he came back with Steven. He spotted me with a group of pretty friends and had to make his appearance. Chloe said, "Why don't we go to my parent's bar, The Lucky Leprechaun?" Brian screamed out that he was in love. Brian was always so dramatic. Chloe replied, "So, that's a plan. We'll meet up at my father's bar, The Lucky Leprechaun, in Bensonhurst.

Slim was trying to get out of it, but Emma jumped in and told her not to worry. Since she was with them, Connor wouldn't mind. That put Slim at ease. She tried to act like that wasn't the reason she hadn't wanted to go, but we all knew better. I suspected it, but Emma confirmed it. Slim really didn't like crowds because of what happened to her. She was also submissive to the men she dated in the past. Christie was also bored. She was single and ready to mingle.

Everyone was excited, especially Brian. He is a Staten Island boy and loved to get out of the borough. He was also the player of the team. He was the "go to" guy. I had to drop the twins home so I was glad that we had taken separate cars.

Kat drove with Ryan, and Steven went with Brian and the other teammates. I left with the twins. Prince was nagging all the way home because he wanted to have more fun. I told him he would have plenty of time for fun when he got my age, and then he wouldn't want to be anywhere near us. I explained to him that kids his age were not even allowed to go in where we were going. He joked about him being tall and that he could pass as an adult.

Princess turned around and said that adults could be boring and catty. I knew she was talking about what she observed during the course of the day. I told Princess that this was why I kept my circle of friends small. Princess was ready to enjoy her weekend with her older cousin Tracey, so she really didn't care about my plans. Princess reminded me that Tracey was coming over and that she could drive.

Tracey had taken the twins under her wings like I had taken her under my wings. Prince's mood changed once he realized Tracey was bringing her best friend Tabatha. Prince had a crush on Tabatha. His face lit up with joy.

I took a quick shower and changed. I wore black fitted stretch jeans, a black tank top, over the knee boots, and a light red short jacket. I wore my hair down and put on my favorite nude color lip gloss. Tracey came into my room while I was getting dressed and asked me who I was getting sexy for. She rolled her eyes playfully and said, "I know, Steven." We both started to laugh. I loved to see Tracey smile, even if her laughter was at my expense. I replied "Yes," I was ready to see my baby Steven.

I kissed everyone and left the house. My mom kissed me and told me to page her when I met up with my friends. I assured her I would. I didn't like to worry her. It was only 25 minutes to The Lucky Leprechaun. They had a parking lot for their customers, which was a plus for me.

Steven spotted little ole me as soon as I walked into the bar. His friends were poking fun at him. They teased him about how much he was in love with me. We all laughed and Kat sort of came to his rescue. She told his friends that he better be in love with me. Connor was there also with a couple of his buddies. Steven was glad to see me. He got nervous around crowds where he had to socialize. People really don't know this. Steven appears relaxed, but most of the time he's lost, unless there is some form of structure. He needs at least one person around that he was familiar with.

Everyone was having a good time. It was like we had all grown up together. I saw how happy Slim was. Slim didn't expect today to turn out like this. She had been walking on eggshells and now we were all having fun and relaxing. I noticed Chloe was getting cozy with Brian. I laughed because Brian might be chewing off more than he could handle. She was not one of those easy-going Italian girls that he was used too. Chloe could run circles around Brian. I was ready to see the outcome of this relationship.

The place was lively, and the music was loud. I noticed a person from their neighborhood coming into the bar; he must have just gotten off work. Some of the workers were blue collar and others were white collar. They were from the neighborhood and came together for laughs.

Steven and his friends stood out like sore thumbs.

They all had their team jackets on. Their game was televised, so people knew who they were. I began to think that maybe Emma had an alternative motive for inviting Steven and his friends to the bar. Our table was getting more crowded by the minute. We were meeting Connor's friends and other relatives. I felt like we were meeting all of Ireland. Now I knew how other people felt at my family functions.

I noticed there was this old man sitting by himself. He sat in a corner. He looked like he was in his early 60s. He was well dressed. He wore a suit. He had a newspaper and a notebook with pen in his hand. He must be a regular because the bartender knew what he wanted without him having to ask. There was a cane next to his seat. People greeted him but didn't sit next to him. He looked lonely to me.

I whispered in Steven's ear to look at the old man sitting by himself. Steven looked at him and said we should buy him a drink. I called the waitress over to order more hot wings, a cheese stake, fries, and whatever the older lonely-looking man was drinking.

We were laughing without a care in the world and the waitress walked over to Steven and said Nick (the older man we had bought a drink) wanted to speak to us. We had forgotten about the gesture, but we walked over to the table where Mr. Nick was sitting.

Mr. Nick invited us to get comfortable and have a seat. He had a thick accent and I barely understood him. He asked us if we were from around here. He knew we weren't from around there, but we decided to humor him and responded with respect. I told him I lived in Flatbush and Steven told him that he was from Georgia.

We asked him where was he from. He looked uncomfortable that we had asked him personal questions. I think he felt insulted, but quickly smiled to hide his distain. I thought to myself maybe Mr. Nick is not a lonely old man. Maybe he is just a cranky old man. He said he was from Russia. He asked Steven what brought him to New York City. Steven answered school and basketball. He realized he was talking to an older person, so he rephrased his answer. He told him that he was playing basketball for his college. Mr. Nick wanted to know more about Stevens's game and score.

Mr. Nick offered to buy us drinks. We told him that we were drinking soda. He smiled and signaled the waitress to come over to order our soda. I noticed that his paper was opened to the sports section. Mr. Nick had gone from a quiet man, sitting in the corner, to an old man that wouldn't stop talking.

People kept coming to the table and he kept telling them, "Later," and they all apologized for disturbing him. I asked Mr. Nick if he wanted us to leave, and he replied "No," and that we weren't going anywhere. I thought that was rude.

I really wanted to go join our table. I started to feel uncomfortable. I kept thinking to myself, "No good deed goes unpunished." We had been sitting with him for about 30 minutes, but it felt like forever. I usually liked speaking to new people, but Mr. Nick was vague and evasive. He didn't talk much about himself. He was also intrusive in a weird way.

Steven didn't appear to mind; his answers were superficial. He was used to strangers asking a million questions. Chloe walked over to the table acting sillier than usual. She smiled and asked Nicholas (Mr. Nick) if she could have her friends back. Mr. Nick's smile was wide, but insincere, and he responded with "Sure." He told us he would be seeing us. I kept thinking I hope not.

We returned to our table. At the end of the night everyone exchanged telephone and beeper numbers and promised to keep in contact. Chloe and Brian acted like they had known each other for forever. Chloe was giggling while Brian was whispering in her ear. They were both drunk and happy. This was the first time I had seen Slim and Connor interact in a social setting.

Slim was a little timid and shy, while Connor was protective and kind towards her. Slim deserved someone kind like him. Slim deserved everything good. I was happy for her. It seemed like fate had been kind to all three of us. It was a good feeling hanging out with everyone and everyone getting along. I felt like my circle was growing. Steven drove home with me and Brian drove the rest of the team home. Kat left with Ryan. Slim drove Stacey and Christie home, while the others helped their father close The Lucky Leprechaun.

As we were leaving the bar, Mr. Nick called us over to his table. He joked about us leaving and not coming over to say goodbye. I honestly forgot all about him. We just smiled and we both said "No" at the same time. Mr. Nick promised to come and watch Steven play. He handed him his card and advised him to call if he ever needed anything. I thought it was strange for Mr. Nick to make such a nice gesture, but Steven was used to it.

Steven was used to having older, male role models or just having them being interested in his games. He had so many unofficial coaches and mentors. He saw it as a blessing. That's how he met his Uncle Jerome. Jerome mentored Steven and his brother throughout the years. He was the one to suggest they get into sports.

Mr. Jerome mentioned that their father was a very good athlete. He went to their games. He was a science teacher. He didn't even play sports and had never been a coach. Their Uncle Jerome knew their father and uncle and said they were natural athletes.

Their Uncle Jerome was always calculating and dealt with facts. He didn't really have a charismatic personality. He had a dry sense of humor. It hadn't really mattered to them because they appreciated and love him unconditionally.

Steven loved him more then they loved their Uncle Nelson. He was the best thing since sliced bread to them. He was particular, but his plans always worked, and his intentions were good. Their Uncle Nelson never really liked their Uncle Jerome, he just tolerated him. Nelson always thought Jerome was an odd bird. He didn't like or feel comfortable around Jerome or his family.

Nelson would advise Steven to be careful. Nelson would tell them that no matter what, blood was thicker than water. Steven secretly thought that his Uncle Nelson was jealous of his Uncle Jerome's relationship with them and the involvement in their lives. His Uncle Nelson would invite Jerome and his family for dinner because of them. Jerome would do the same, but he always appeared genuine.

Jerome's house was huge and looked like something out of a magazine. Not one thing was ever misplaced not even in his kid's rooms. Jerome's sons, Kenneth, and Kevin loved when Steven and his brother would come over. They thought Steven and his brother were fun and they didn't get into trouble. I always thought that statement was odd, but Steven couldn't see any wrongdoings by his Uncle Jerome.

Jerome was a saint that they needed when times were rough. I felt that kids aren't supposed to be in constant fear of their parents. Jerome kids was always afraid of making mistakes. There was always plenty of food, but it was bland. It was always a little awkward when the two families had dinner together. Jerome offered to take family vacations together, but that never happened.

Mr. Nelson would say he didn't want to go anywhere with them, but he really couldn't afford family vacations. Mr. Nelson was a hard-working blue-collar man who never accepted handouts. Steven respected his Uncle Nelson for that. His uncle Nelson told Steven that nothing in life was free.

Mr. Nelson never understood where Mr. Jerome got all the money he had. A teacher's salary couldn't buy all the things that Mr. Jerome had. Steven's Uncle Nelson advised him to be very selective in accepting help from people. Steven remembered that advice whenever people offered him gifts or money because of his basketball skills. Steven was a little guarded and he took his uncle's advice.

The drive home was fast. There were hardly any cars

on the road. Steven was happy that his teammates and my friends met up at The Lucky Leprechaun. This was the first time that Steven had met Slim and Connor. He thought Slim was nice. He mentioned that she appeared shy and wasn't as outgoing as Kat and me.

I had never mentioned the ordeal that Slim had gone through. I had never told anyone about what Steven confided in me. I tried not to betray the trust that my friends and family had in me. I never exposed what happened to them that had made them vulnerable.

I remembered that we had a full house so I called Amelia to ask if Steven could spend the night. My mom said it was okay, but he would have to sleep on the couch in my room. I had no problem with that, and I knew Steven would be okay with it. I wanted him to meet Aunt Nene and my cousin Tracey.

Aunt Nene, Tracey and Steven had all heard of each other from me, but they had never met each other. Whenever I described them to each other, I felt so blessed to have such amazing people near me. Amelia was up when we got there.

Amelia always stayed up and didn't go to sleep until I made it home. Amelia greeted us and asked if we were hungry and questioned if we had fun. We both stated that we were full. I told her I had fun and that Slim's future in-laws weren't too bad. I told Amelia about the family bar and that strange old foreign man, Mr. Nick. Amelia just smiled and joked about him being a mobster. She went to bed and left us in the kitchen.

Steven and I talked for about 15 more minutes and then headed to my room. I took my Tweety Bird pajamas and headed to the bathroom to change and let Steven change in the room. Steven always had a pair of sweatpants and a t-shirt at my house. I washed it when I did my laundry. He spent a lot of time here since he had no family in New York City.

After changing, we talked for most of the night. We talked about the future. We talked about school. I talked about the medical school I planned to attend and my hopes of getting accepted. Steven had major decisions to make. He definitely planned on getting his undergraduate degree and going to medical school. There was a 90 percent chance that he would be recruited for the National Basketball Association (NBA). He knew that there was a strong chance he would have to move out of state.

Steven asked me if I would move with him if that was the case. He mentioned that there were good medical schools everywhere. He planned on retiring in his mid 30's and going back to medical school himself. I told him that I couldn't move in with someone unless I was married. He just smiled and hugged me.

I felt special; he had told me that he only talked about his future with his brother and uncles. Now, he found himself talking more to me about his future. He wanted me to be part of his life and I was his future. He tried not to get too excited about his future in front of other people. We talked until we fell asleep.

We awoke to the smell of bacon and sausage. Amelia was making breakfast for everyone. Everybody was already up, watching television and playing around in the living room. I introduced my cousin Tracey and her best friend to Steven. Tracey couldn't help but smile. That's usually people's first reaction when they see Steven.

Tracey blurted out, "You are so tall." We all started laughing. This was the usual second reaction to seeing Steven. I was happy Tracey was enjoying herself and acting like a silly teenager. That was something I always wanted for her.

It wasn't easy for Tracey. It had taken a lot of family support and many therapy sessions to get her to where she was today. The therapy allowed her to feel less anxious and reminded her that she is loved. She forgot some of her pain and stopped acting like a middle-aged black man who had been raised in segregation. Her hurt and mistrust of people was so deep.

Prince quickly took over the conversation with Steven. Steven was the older brother Prince never had. I was happy that Steven was a positive role model to Prince. I never brought anyone I dated, other than Keith, near my family. Keith was just a friend when he came around. He came only once and that was for my junior high school graduation party.

Steven didn't mind because this was his chance to act like an older brother. Prince always showed Steven off to his friends. We usually laughed and acted like we didn't know what he was doing. Steven didn't mind because he was used to it.

I left everyone to go help Amelia with breakfast. Amelia was making breakfast and prepping for dinner at the same time. She was cleaning and seasoning the meat, which I took over. We were having griot w/mushroom rice and shrimp. This was one of the Haitian's favorite dishes. Americans who tasted it loved it too.

Amelia was an excellent cook, and everyone loved her food. The doorbell rang and I quickly washed my hands to go answer it. It was my Aunt Nene. I knew she was coming over and I had been excited about it. I kissed her on her cheek and started pulling on her to go towards the living room. I looked like a kid pulling on her mother. I wanted her to finally meet Steven.

Aunt Nene was smiling like usual and told me to go ahead while she spoke to Amelia for a little while. I looked at her for a second out of concern and Aunt Nene told me nothing was wrong, and she'd be there in a few minutes. I ran to the living room to tell everyone that she was here. Everyone was happy and excited. Aunt Nene was the fun aunt. I watched Tracey's reaction to everyone's reaction to Aunt Nene. She looked proud of her mother and finally saw her mother the way I had always seen her. Aunt Nene was and continued to be amazing.

Aunt Nene walked into the living room with Amelia. I ran and grabbed her hand to bring her nearer to Steven. Steven stood up to greet Aunt Nene and she told him he didn't have to stand up. She went to sit next to him.

Aunt Nene picked up on his accent immediately. She asked him what part of Georgia he was from. He told her he was from Woodland, Georgia. Aunt Nene quickly told him she was from Manchester, Georgia, which was a neighboring city. Aunt Nene was born and raised in Manchester.

They were both shocked and pleased about the coincidence. They hugged each other like they were lost relatives. The two cities were sports rivals. Aunt Nene wanted to know more about Steven's family. Steven told her the names of his parents and uncle.

Aunt Nene knew of his father and uncle. They had played sports, and they had been really good. They were her town rivals when it came to sports, but they were good. They were laughing and then she started looking at Steven with pitiful eyes. I knew she knew that Steven's mother died, and his father had run off. She didn't mention it in front of anyone.

I felt sheer joy being surrounded by my family and a loving boyfriend. I was happy that everyone loved Steven and he loved my family. We stayed in all day and listened to Aunt Nene stories about Georgia. Steven was listening to her like she was reading his favorite bedtime story. I watched Steven sitting there with my Aunt Nene; I could never have imagined all that was happening.

My life changed for the better with little effort. My Aunt Nene has been drug free for over a decade. Her face had started to fill in and she was looking more beautiful than ever. She started to look like she had in her old pictures. Her skin was glowing. She was not too thin or heavy. His hair was bouncing with curls. She was an inspiration.

THE BIG GAME

Chloe and I were becoming very close since she started dating Brian. She would come to St. John's University basketball games with me. Chloe attended the games to support and watch Brian play. We would sometimes go for lunch together and regularly talked on the telephone. Chloe even sat in one of my classes with me once. She was thinking about enrolling at St. John's. Chloe even spoke to Kat on the telephone.

I saw Chloe more frequently than I saw Slim lately. Chloe and I had our routine. We would go to St. John's games to watch Steven and Brian play and then head out to The Lucky Leprechaun to celebrate whether they won or lost. Some of the regulars at The Lucky Leprechaun started coming to the games. Chloe hung a group picture at The Lucky Leprechaun that had been taken at one of St. John's basketball games.

Mr. Nick even showed up to a couple of those games with a couple of other men with weird accents like his. He introduced them to Steven at the game.

Brian had already met Mr. Nick's friends and was speaking to them like they were long, lost relatives. They were even giving him pointers on his jump shots. The two men that accompanied Mr. Nick were huge. You could see their muscles through their clothing. They were dressed in dark designer suits like Mr. Nick.

They stuck out like sore thumbs at the basketball game. Everyone else was casually dressed. We figured Brian had met them at The Lucky Leprechaun while hanging out with Chloe. Brian hung out at The Lucky Leprechaun a lot. Mr. Nick would always speak to us and buy us food. We would return the favor and buy him his favorite drink. That was another routine.

I started to see Brian sitting at Mr. Nick's table from time to time. Their conversation appeared to be friendly and they were all smiles. I tried to act like I didn't notice it. The less I knew about Old Nick, the better. My experience taught me that when things looked strange, they are usually strange. I didn't want to ask questions because that was Steven's friend and Chloe's boyfriend.

Chloe was going to be part of Slim's family, and it would be hard to avoid her if things got messy because of my assumptions. I could be 100 percent honest with Kat, but I still didn't know Chloe that well. I knew Slim wanted her fairy tale life at all costs and I respected that.

Chloe and Brian looked like they were madly in love. They had been inseparable since they met. Brian stopped letting groupies hang around him at school. He was always talking about how amazing and beautiful Chloe was. He appeared to change in more ways than one. Some changes were for the better and other behaviors appeared odd.

Brian started having extra money, driving cars, and being flashy. He never disclosed how he got the money and cars, and we never asked. Steven admitted to me that Mr. Nick's friend had tried to get too friendly with him. It made him feel uncomfortable.

They approached Steven twice. The first time was after practice. The coach noticed how uncomfortable he was and told Steven to go run some laps around the gym. The second time they approached Steven he was using the bathroom at The Lucky Leprechaun. Steven played dumb. He never used the bathroom at The Lucky Leprechaun again.

They were asking him about his average score and how much did he think he could score at the next game. They asked him if he could score less than usual. That reminded Steven of a conversation he had with Brian. The questions were too similar to dismiss it as a coincidence. They asked Steven about his average score and what would happen if he didn't score that high or didn't win a game. Would not scoring so high really hurt him?

They mentioned that he was a good player. Could he guess how much he would score the next time he played? Steven noticed that Brian hadn't been playing his best games after asking those questions. They would win but he knew Brian was not doing his best. Steven thought that Brian was into gambling. We just couldn't figure out why. Brian attended St. John's on a basketball scholarship, but his parents could easily afford to pay his tuition.

Brian came from an upper middle-class family. Brian's mother was a successful cooperate attorney. His father was an established championship high school coach at St. Peters. His parents were both alumni of St. John's University, which is where they had met. He had two older siblings that graduated from St. John's. They were not athletic like him and his dad.

Brian had more than most college students. I didn't know why he was dealing with Old Nick and his associates. Steven and I started calling Mr. Nick "Old Nick" because of his negative vibe. I heard his two companions were dangerous and part of the Russian mob.

Brian was the person you'd go to if you needed

anything. He knew where and who to go to for anything. He showed the other team members around. All the freshman basketball players looked up to him. Steven stayed clear of the new car Brian was driving. The other team members would jump in the car, but Steven made excuses not to get in. Steven disclosed that he had seen other teammates in high school get caught up in illicit activities once their popularity rose. He didn't want any part of it.

St. John's had a winning streak. They were number one in the National Collegiate Athlete Association (NCA). They practiced hard and worked great as a team. They even beat Georgetown.

Their coach had a lucky sweater that he would wear at every game. Their games were always full. They were getting so much attention that St. John's repaired the basketball court. The floor was shiny. St. John's was written in red letters in the middle of the court. The seats were red. The gym was beautiful. The team was given new uniforms. They played well and they were being rewarded for it with all the attention. There were plenty of articles written about the team.

Their games were bringing in fans from all over. They had people coming from all five boroughs and neighboring cities and states cheering them on. Steven stayed the same throughout his team's success.

His uncles and brothers called more often to say how proud they were of him. They all planned on coming to the championship game to support him. I spoke to his brother, Damian, a couple of times. They sounded similar. They were both passionate about sports when they spoke. His brother would tease him about being a superstar. Steven would reply that he was trying to be like him. His brother was one of the top five college football quarterbacks. He was also doing great.

Steven continued to study hard in school and spent all of his spare time with me and my family. He admitted to me that he didn't think he could have made it without my support. He was feeling lonely at St. John's despite always being surrounded by a crowd. He had his brother and uncles in Georgia. He even missed his Uncle Nelson. He always appreciated him, but never thought he would miss him.

Steven told me that he knew there was something special about me. He never wanted someone around, just to have someone around. He wanted his friendships and relationships to be meaningful. Steven spent so many years on the outside looking in. He had plenty of time to decide what he wanted out of life and what kinds of people he wanted around him.

People spoke around Steven like he was invisible since he was a loner. They probably thought who he was going to tell. They never imagined that he would grow up to be this talented basketball player.

Steven saw how people hurt each other when they were not genuine. He also heard the stories about his parents. People didn't take notice of him until his freshman year of high school. His basketball skills surpassed his older teammates. He was playing varsity freshman year.

I didn't remind him of any girls from back home. That made me special to him. He said I look focused, confident, and unbothered by what was going on around me. He said I moved without a care in the world and I didn't appear to worry about who was watching me. He noticed this about me since the first day of class. He thought to himself that I was going to be his girlfriend. He was happy when we had several classes together.

He said that gave him more of an opportunity to get to know me. He didn't date a lot in high school. He admitted to me that I didn't make it easy for him. I didn't throw myself at him when I heard he played basketball. I told him that I was happy we started dating, and he had won me over at the bookstore. I looked forward to seeing him in classes. His kindness made me see him differently. Steven just replied that he would have done anything to get to know me. He would do anything for me.

I just smiled as we drove back to Brooklyn. We had some of our deepest, heart-felt conversations in the car. I felt like I had known Steven all of my life. I couldn't wait for us to get back home to study and relax.

It took us 30 minutes to find parking three blocks away from the building. We were still grateful. We didn't have class for the rest of the week and Steven was done with practice for the week. Our biggest plan was to study for our chemistry test.

We got to the house and I saw Tracey sitting on the couch with Princess. I knew something was wrong because Tracey was fighting back tears and it was a Wednesday. Tracey usually came over on the weekend because of school.

Steven must have picked up on it too and he just looked at me. I told him maybe he should go put his duffle bag in my room. I went and sat next to Tracey and just hugged her. She put her head down on my chest and told me that her mother was in the hospital again.

Aunt Nene has lupus. Aunt Nene's mother, my grandmother, had lupus. My grandmother had a high-risk pregnancy. That's how my grandmother died. We all knew that, so we always got scared when Aunt Nene had a flare up. Aunt Nene's lupus caused her to have seizures. She wore a medical alert bracelet all the time.

The medical alert bracelet has her medical information, emergency contact, and her primary care physician's information. Tracey always takes it the hardest. Aunt Nene tried to calm everyone's fears whenever she is admitted to the hospital. She always assures us she will be okay even when she is not. The good thing is that she was at Kings County Hospital.

My mom worked at Kings County Hospital and could go and see her, even after visiting hours. Amelia sometimes spent the night at the hospital. Amelia usually saw her before and after work. I made some tea to relax everyone's nerves. Haitian people drink tea for any type of ailment and emotional distress. They drink it as a preventative measure. Every leaf has its purpose.

I went to the room and spoke to Steven about what happened to my Aunt Nene. He gave me a hug because he knew how sensitive I am and how much I love all my aunts. I cried and I felt like I released a ton of anxiety off my shoulders. This was the first time I cried around someone since I was 13-years old. I usually went to my room and played my music loud to drown out my crying.

I never felt comfortable letting my tears flow in front of anyone. I was surrounded by strong women and I just didn't cry in front of people. I was usually the person telling everyone that everything would be okay. I'm usually the one doing the cheering up of people around me and keeping things calm and peaceful.

Steven asked me if he should leave because he didn't want to impose. I told him it was okay, and he could stay. The more normal things appeared the better it would be for Tracey. Aunt Nene usually pulled through. I also told him that we had made plans to study. I told him that he could start without me because I was going to start dinner. I was going to make Aunt Nene's favorite meal, which was lasagna and garlic knots. I smiled and told Steven I would make his favorite desert. He smiled.

Steven cannot resist carrot cake. Steven let out a goofy, childish laugh. His laugh made me laugh. This is what I loved about our relationship. We were always trying to make each other happy. Everything he had gone through and everything I experienced made us good for each other. It was funny how we still taught each other new things.

I changed into comfortable sweatpants and a t-shirt. I asked Princess and Tracey to come help me in the kitchen. This was our regular routine. We used to rush to the hospital but realized it's better to bring Aunt Nene some food. I know Amelia was checking on her. She was in good hands in the hospital. We played music and imitated the latest and legendary musicians as we cooked and cleaned.

I tried to keep Tracey occupied whenever Aunt Nene got sick. The only person missing was Prince. Tracey didn't come, so I had to playfully push her into the kitchen. That made her laugh because I used to carry her when she was smaller. This was our routine, but now she was taller than me.

Tracey looked like a model. She was very beautiful, and she knew it. She's not shallow or anything, she just knew her worth and what she wanted out of life. She kind of reminded me of a young Kat. I knew once I got Tracey into the kitchen, she would cheer up.

We always cook for Aunt Nene to cheer her up. It made us feel useful. She always acted like she loved our cooking, even when we didn't know how to cook very well. I turned on the radio and began cutting onions, garlic, and scallions. Tracey was taking out the pots for the sauce and pasta.

We were getting in the grove and then the Michael Jackson song "Beat It" came on the radio. We stopped everything and started singing the song and tried to break dance. We were just acting silly without a care in the world, like usual. Next thing we knew, Steven added himself to our three-women show. He was in the middle, break dancing and be-bopping to the music. Tracey, Princess, and I didn't stop or skip a beat. We were being silly, goofy, and having fun. After the song was over, we all started laughing.

Steven asked if he could help us in anyway. We looked at each other and laughed, and I quickly said I thought he had never cooked before. He laughed and said he had magic fingers and could do anything with them. I laughed and said, "Okay Houdini. How about you start on the cake batter?" Tracey seconded it. He sat down and then said he understood that we left him with the most important job. Dessert is the best part of the menu.

Steven stayed in the kitchen with us talking and telling jokes. He had us laughing. Prince came home from basketball practice. He poked his head in the kitchen and saw Tracey cooking and knew what happened. He hugged us all and asked what we were cooking. Prince actually said, "Please don't burn the house down." Steven told Prince how he was keeping an eye on us. Prince laughed and joked around a little. He went to take a shower and change out of his sweaty clothes.

We were finished cooking by the time Prince got dressed. We packed up the food and were on our way to the Kings County Hospital. It took us 15 minutes to find street parking.

Tracey knew what room her mother was in. We knew our way around because we were always there. We were either visiting my mom or Aunt Nene at the hospital. We decided to separate into two separate groups. Sometimes the newer security officers would get strict if they saw too many visitors. The twins went in with Tracey and the food. Steven and I followed 15 minutes later.

Aunt Nene was happy to see all of us. She looked a little pale and had a grayish complexion. She thanked all of us for cooking the food. She loved it. Just seeing her happy made us all feel a little at ease. That was the reason we cooked, to bring a smile to her face. We must have been laughing too much because we didn't hear the nurse when she walked in the room. I immediately gave her an "Uh oh, we got caught" face. She gave me a stern look and then smiled. I already knew Nurse Smith.

Nurse Smith used to work on the same floor with my mom. She had been expecting the crowd. Nurse Smith admitted the smell of the food gave us away. It was a change from the hospital's usual funny smell. They used heavy chemicals like Iodoform to stop the spread of germs. Iodoform has a distinct smell.

The other nurses on that floor were expecting us too. We always did this. If it was possible, they always give Aunt Nene her own room. They knew she would have more visitors than most. We sometimes spent the night at the hospital.

The room was an average single person hospital room. It had a bathroom. There was a window facing the busy streets of Brooklyn. The room was cold. The walls were painted beige with a green flowered wallpaper design at the bottom of the walls. Nurse Smith gave me a hug and told me that she had seen Amelia earlier today. Nurse Smith just wanted to say hi to us before she left.

Steven looked at us and smiled. He called us the "Trouble Jones Clan." We all just smiled, and I said we would do anything for family. Family is number one. Steven smiled but he looked sad. Aunt Nene must have noticed it, so she asked him about his big game. Steven was acting shy. Aunt Nene smiled and said, "You didn't think I forgot about it. Even if I did, it's all over the news. I watch the news. I've seen your televised games." He was blushing.

Aunt Nene complimented him about his game. Steven told her he was okay. Steven is not good at taking compliments. I found that adorable about him. Aunt Nene asked Steven about his uncles and older brother. Steven told us that he was so excited that his brother and uncles were coming to watch him play.

His Uncle Jerome planned the trip and made all the arrangements. It killed his Uncle Nelson that his Uncle Jerome was paying for everything, but he was coming anyway. His Uncle Jerome had wanted to visit him much sooner.

Aunt Nene mentioned how she couldn't wait to see his Uncle Nelson. She was surprised that she didn't know his Uncle Jerome. She even knew Jerome's wife, but not him. The two towns were so small that everyone either knew each other or knew of each other. Aunt Nene smiled and said she couldn't wait to meet him. He seemed like an interesting person. Steven laughed and replied, "That he is."

Amelia walked into the hospital room after her shift was over. She asked, "Who is coming over?" I told Amelia that we were talking about Steven's Uncle Jerome. Amelia was glad that Steven's family was coming. Amelia went to kiss Aunt Nene and we all hugged Amelia.

Aunt Nene was happy to see all of us there. She acted surprised about the food even though we did this same routine every time. She asked who baked the cake and I pointed at Steven. She said it wasn't bad. Amelia had a sweet tooth. Amelia took a piece of cake and smiled; she nodded with satisfaction at Steven.

Steven mentioned that his family couldn't wait to meet all of us. His Uncle Nelson was happy that he was dating me and had found a nice family to look after him. His Uncle Jerome, on the other hand, wanted to know more details about everyone and everything that Steven did. He asked about my mom, the twins, Aunt Nene, and Tracey. He didn't want Steven to leave out any details. Jerome was overly happy as if he was living through Steven. He was concerned and very protective of Steven. He had been that way for years.

We were all looking forward to meeting them in two weeks. I was nervous, even though I acted like I wasn't. I thought about what could happen if they didn't like me or if I didn't like them. I usually didn't get close to my boyfriend's family. This was actually my first real relationship, maybe my first real love. I didn't share my fear about meeting his family with him.

I thought about how hard it was for him to meet my family and friends. My family was not even from the same country as him. Our culture was different, and it didn't scare him away. I must have been deep in thoughts because I didn't see Kat when she entered the hospital room. She hugged and kissed Aunt Nene and then sat on my lap. There weren't any places left for her to sit. We were expecting more people. Aunt Nene's coworkers, friends, and my other aunts would be coming by.

Aunt Nene had made a lot of caring and supportive friends over the years. Once she had recovered and stopped using drugs, she helped everyone she came in contact with. Kat whispered that she had something to tell me about Chloe, The Lucky Leprechaun, and Brian. My facial expression gave her the look that I wouldn't be surprised. I'm concerned, but not surprised. I told her that I had something to tell her too.

More people came to visit Aunt Nene, so I decided to leave to make more room. I would be back tomorrow.

Prince, Steven, and Kat left with me. Kat hadn't driven up there. I was glad that Princess and Tracey had stayed with Amelia.

Amelia could take care of herself, but I was glad she wouldn't be coming home late by herself. I was trying to catch up with what was new in Kat's life without really going deep in conversation. Kat had been busy with school, Ryan, and R.J. We hadn't had a chance to catch up. I was guilty of being busy with studying, family issues, and Steven. I had even let Chloe distract me from hanging with my best friend.

Kat and I were sitting in front making small talk, and Prince and Steven were sitting in the back. I don't think they were even listening to us. They were talking about basketball and were planning on playing a game once we get home. I knew Steven wanted to get one quick game out of his system before he started to study. That would give me a great time to catch up and hear what Kat had to say about Chloe and The Lucky Leprechaun.

We parked and we all went into the building. I told Steven and Prince that I would be at Kat's house. They didn't care, they had basketball on their minds. Steven loved showing Prince new things and Prince loved learning so he could try new moves out at his games.

Steven had attended a few of Prince's games. Prince's coaches were excited to meet Steven. Prince's coach didn't need any introduction when he saw Steven. Prince hadn't expected that his teammates and coach would make such a big deal about Steven coming to the game. He just wanted Steven to see him play. They bonded over basketball and food. Half of the time it was like I wasn't even there. I loved the way they bonded with each other.

There was no one at Kat's apartment. We had privacy but Kat still closed the door just in case her mother walked in. Chloe kept calling Kat because she knew Kat was studying business law. Kat thought that was weird that Chloe came to her because Brian's mother was actually a practicing business attorney.

Chloe was being vague, but she wanted to know about business partnerships. She wanted to know more about silent partners and how to dissolve a partnership; how to sell and repurchase a business, while keeping the business' name.

Chloe wanted to know different ways to dissolve a partnership with the least amount of consequences for the original business owner. She would not go into detail, but Kat guessed she was talking about her family's business.

Kat didn't force any information out of her but told her she needed more details in order to help her. Chloe said to forget it. She said she was asking because of a business proposition that she was offered. Chloe wanted to know how to dissolve it just in case she wanted to. Kat had met a handful of attorneys when she was an intern. She had several practicing attorneys and judges as professors. Kat really wanted to help but didn't want to push or ruin anything for Slim.

Slim probably knew what was going on but hadn't disclosed any information to us. We loved Slim, but she never saw things for what they were and was willing to blame others for her unhappiness. Sometimes other people were at fault, but, sometimes, it was because of her failure to see things for what they were.

Kat wanted to know what was going on with Chloe's family business. Kat figured Chloe opened the door for it. She asked a classmate of hers that worked in the County Clerk's office to look up ownership of The Lucky Leprechaun.

Kat's friend found out that The Lucky Leprechaun had almost gone out of business three years ago. Slim's future in-laws had begun filing for bankruptcy. Then, out of nowhere, their debt was cleared. According to tax documents, The Lucky Leprechaun grossed less then when they filed for bankruptcy three years ago.

This explained why Slim's grandparents were paying for the entire wedding. Conner's parents didn't have the money. Slim's grandparents had always given her anything she wanted. They would do anything to make her happy.

Connor's parents appeared to have money but did not. They owned a big, beautiful house, a business, foreign cars, and were always going on cruises. It seemed like Chloe's parents were into something that they had welcomed at first but were now trying to sever ties. My mouth dropped because the business was dirty.

Kat did not stop with this information. She asked Ryan if he had heard about any illegal activities going on at The Lucky Leprechaun; more than the normal illegal activities going on in any NYC bar. Ryan discovered that there was an active, ongoing investigation of the bar. He didn't know any details of the investigation, but he advised us to stay away from the bar. Kat wanted to know if I had heard or seen anything suspicious, since I went to The Lucky Leprechaun on a regular basis.

I told Kat about Old Nick and his suspicious friends or colleagues. I mentioned how they approached Steven on several occasions about his game and scoring. Steven had felt uncomfortable and acted dumb. I mentioned how Brian was driving new cars, flashing money around, and was always at The Lucky Leprechaun.

This information put us in an awkward position. We didn't know whether to mention it to Slim or not. Slim was very secretive and we weren't sure if she already knew or not. We agreed to not mention anything for now. I was more than okay with it because they had kept quiet information about my dad and grandfather in the past. I had been upset at first, but I was glad they did. Kat had been up front with me ever since. She doesn't assume I know anything, and I do the same for her.

Slim is very sensitive and she might have been devastated and jumped to conclusions. Slim lacked the coping skills to deal with this situation. She would ruin her wedding plans and blame it on us. We always looked out for her without her knowledge. She would try to confront Connor and then blame everything on us.

This information should not come from us without hard facts, and we really didn't have many details. Slim and Connor were hardly ever at the bar, so she was sure it would not directly affect her. Slim always distanced herself from anything illegal, and now her prince charming might be linked to the Russian mob. We considered the irony of avoiding danger all of your life, and then ending up married into a family that was affiliated with the Russian mob.

Kat mentioned her annoyance with her current relationship. We also had our own serious problems, such as Aunt Nene being hospitalized, mid-terms, and relationship problems. Slim stopped caring about what was going on in our lives a long time ago. She stopped asking questions or cut us off when we spoke and turn the conversation back to her. Slim acted like our problems were not important. I knew it was because she was still hurt. We were the ones that knew the beautiful child version of herself that she hated so much.

Slim had hated herself for years. Slim hated what happened to her. She hated that she couldn't protect herself. Slim was angry at everyone because of what happened to her. She stopped acting mean because Kat had confronted her. Kat told Slim that what happened to her wasn't our fault, but she acted like she wished it was. There was silence. Slim hadn't cried, got upset, or denied it. That confirmed how she felt about us and probably every girl around her age at that time.

Things had changed between us since then. We were used to it; we understand her and didn't blame her for it. We still felt bad for what happened to her in the past. We were usually there to pick up the pieces. I asked Kat what was new with her.

Kat mentioned that the universe was testing her patience and relationship with Ryan. I asked her what Ryan had done, and she told me it was nothing he had done on purpose. Situations changed and things just got complicated.

R.J.'s mother, Tiffany, moved back to New York City. Tiffany graduated college, missed NYC, and wanted her family back. Tiffany had expected Ryan to welcome her back with open arms. She found a job, started a career she wanted, had her own apartment, but realized that she missed her family.

Ryan had been nervous about telling Kat that Tiffany came back. Ryan told her that his mother had called him to tell him that he had company. His mother told him not to bring R.J. with him. Ryan arrived at his mother's house to see Tiffany standing there smiling.

Tiffany mentioned that she was in town for a couple of months. She was getting herself together. Tiffany was also nervous about speaking to Ryan and seeing R.J. She had decided to speak to Ryan's mother first. She then tried to win favor from Ryan because of her accomplishments.

Ryan claimed that he had no intention of getting back with her, but he was happy that she was back to meet her son. Kat just listened to him speak. She was calm and acted indifferent throughout the conversation. Kat was ready to call it quits right there. Kat really did not like any complications in her life. Kat would have been more understanding if Ryan had been up front with her from the beginning, but he sat on this information for about two weeks.

I told her maybe he was confused and needed to think about it first. Ryan's mother Ms. Dorothy sent him to the store and Kat was the first she told, in confidence, about Tiffany. Ms. Dorothy mentioned how disgusted she was with the situation.

Kat felt like Ms. Dorothy expected an award or a

party for finally doing the right thing. She begged Kat not to break up with Ryan. Ms. Dorothy knew her son would do the right thing. She was also worried about R.J. Kat always thought Ms. Dorothy didn't like her, but her solidarity was with Kat. She didn't like how Tiffany had hurt her son and abandoned her grandson.

Ms. Dorothy admitted that Ryan had been lost, broken, and devastated when Tiffany left. He stopped going to school for a semester, didn't work, he barely showered or ate. He wouldn't speak to anyone but his mother. Ms. Dorothy had been really worried. Ryan was like a stranger, a shell of a man. She thought the next step for him was drugs. At one point, Ms. Dorothy thought he was on drugs. One day R.J. had gone to him and said, "Dada."

A simple word from a one-year-old child changed Ryan. Ryan realized that he was responsible for a small human being that resembled and needed him. Ryan was crying uncontrollably. Ms. Dorothy still could not figure out if they had been tears of happiness or sadness, but that was the last time she saw Ryan cry or feel sorry for himself. The love he had for R.J helped him pull himself together.

Everything he did from that day on was to better the lives of him and his son. He was more selective in his choice of women. A pretty face and ambition were not enough. A woman needed to be compassionate and show empathy towards others. He didn't want a weak woman. He wanted an ambitious woman with a bit of loyalty and wisdom. Ms. Dorothy admitted that she liked Kat.

Kat reminded her of herself when she was younger.

That was why she spoke to Kat and prepared her for the situation. She mentioned that she would not blame Kat if she wanted to leave but reminded her that Ryan was a good man and he loved her very much.

Ryan had not dated anyone after the heartbreak until Kat. He changed for the better. Ryan didn't allow Tiffany to meet R.J. before speaking to Kat. Ryan wanted to introduce Kat and Tiffany to each other at Ms. Dorothy's home. Ms. Dorothy was the buffer for everyone. Ryan was allowing Tiffany into R.J.'s life because of R.J. He did not want to short R.J. out of anything in life.

Kat told Ryan that she understood the situation even though it made her feel uncomfortable. Kat felt that if it worked out with Tiffany, maybe they would get some free time together. Ryan was afraid to tell Kat because the situation had to make sense to him first. He didn't want Kat to leave him, so he was sure to tell her how much he loved her and how much she meant to him. Ryan told Kat that she was family and he couldn't wait for the wedding. Ryan was trying to rush things to prove his love to Kat.

Kat wasn't sure if he was ready. Was he afraid of the situation, of losing her, or just being reminded of past pain? Kat loved R.J., but now that his mom had returned to their lives, it made her see things differently. Ryan was a great guy, but she began wondering if she was with him because she felt sorry for him and R.J.

Kat was crying. For the first time, she was unsure about something. She was scared because life was not going as she planned. She loved Ryan and R.J. Kat was not insecure, but she knew there was a good chance of her getting hurt. Kat was the only child and never had to share anything. Kat barely shared anything with me. I knew how she felt. I felt that way about Keith in junior high school. This was Kat's first heartbreak. She was heartbroken because Ryan held out information on this one sensitive issue. Kat had decided years ago that she wouldn't fight for a spot in any man's life.

I shared my information about Steven's weird Uncle Jerome that he loved so much. I told her that both his uncles and brother were coming to see him. His big game was in two weeks. I would finally get to meet Steven's family. I asked her what she was doing during that time. Kat didn't know if she would be free. We had been talking for so long that I lost track of time.

It was late and I hadn't gotten any studying done. Steven and I both had midterms and we hadn't even begun studying. We were both serious about our grades. I told Kat I had to leave to study. It was sad to leave Kat. I would have spent the entire night at her house if I didn't have to study for my test. I felt so sorry for both Kat and Slim. Slim, at least, didn't know anything and got to enjoy her fairytale.

The apartment was quiet when I got there. I thought everyone was asleep until I looked in the kitchen. Amelia and Steven were sitting at the table talking. I knew they were waiting up for me. I went from one worried person to two worried people. I joined them and clued them in on the information I had learned about The Lucky Leprechaun and Slim's in-laws. Amelia and Steven were shocked. We were glad that Kat had a curious nature.

We all agreed to not go there. We would say we had to study or visit Aunt Nene. I wanted to say something, but it could hurt Kat and Ryan. This was the Russian mob and God knows what else was going on. I kept what Kat was going through to myself. I felt guilty that I was so busy, and I wasn't able to catch up with Kat for a few days. I had to study and see Aunt Nene. I really just wanted to hang out with Kat. I wanted to shop, eat out, discuss what was really going on, and make a plan to fix things.

I couldn't do that because our schedules conflicted because of our midterms. Kat's schedule used to be booked, but she decided to take a step back on a few activities with R.J.

Kat allowed Tiffany to do some of the activities that she had done with R.J. Kat even went along with Tiffany and Ms. Dorothy so R.J. felt more comfortable. Tiffany acted nice and tried to get to know her. Kat was not falling for her fake kindness because of their first encounter. Kat acted cordial, but she still resented Tiffany and could not understand how she could abandon R.J. She resented the thought of Tiffany coming back, trying to replace her, and acting like everything was okay. She knew Tiffany wanted Ryan back.

Kat knew there could never really be any true friendship between them. Kat thought that Tiffany was sneaky. Tiffany had tried to act aggressive toward Kat when they first met. Kat pulled her to the side and set her straight. Kat made sure to tell her that she didn't play with man, woman, or child. Tiffany acted shocked, as if she hadn't done anything to Kat.

Ms. Dorothy was happy that Kat stood up for herself. Ms. Dorothy informed Kat that Tiffany was looking for sympathy after that incident. Tiffany hadn't gotten any sympathy from Ryan or Ms. Dorothy. Kat still felt uneasy about everything, despite their loyalty. She didn't disclose how she felt to Ryan or his mother. R.J. got confused with certain interactions he had with Tiffany. I couldn't imagine being in her shoes. It validated how Kat felt, but I reminded her that she had support from Ryan and his mother. I told her I supported her in whatever decision she made because she was my friend.

The days were going fast, and it was getting closer to Steven's game and his family's visit. Steven was very excited about his family's visit and I acted as if I was too. I wanted to support him emotionally like he did for me. I was nervous. We aced our midterms so that was one less thing to worry about.

Unfortunately, Aunt Nene was still in Kings County Hospital. We visited her often and planned different fun activities with Tracey and the twins so they could be more relaxed. They even enjoyed going to Steven's practices. There were news crews and reporters at Steven's practices. The city was excited about it.

I had never paid basketball any attention prior to dating Steven. Everything was going perfect until a week before the game. The coach announced that Brian and three other players would not be playing in the championship game. Brian and two of the other players were starters.

The coach did not give a reason for them not playing. The team was bummed out. This game was very important to them all. The coach gave them a speech that they could do it. He had some plays to practice that would make up for the four players that couldn't play.

Some of the players were willing and ready to replace

Brian and the other players. This was their shot to show the world what they got. Steven told me about the four players; we thought they were caught gambling. There were rumors about what happened all around the campus.

Steven decided to page Brian and I called Chloe. Chloe sounded nervous and said she would catch up with me later and that she couldn't talk to me right then. She said she missed me at The Lucky Leprechaun, and she was sorry about my aunt being sick. I told her I missed her to and asked her if she would be at the game. She giggled and said, "Of course." I had gotten used to her and Brian.

Brian visited Steven at his dorm room. I was already there. He came inside the room like a burglar. Brian was wearing a black skully hat and a sweatshirt with a hood. He appeared calmer than expected. I expected him to be depressed and distraught. He was calm and I told him that I spoke with Chloe and I would meet up with her soon. Brian asked Steven if he heard that he was not playing. Steven said yes that the coach had told the team.

Brian apologized and said he would explain everything in due time. Brian did disclose that the NCAA was investigating him and the other three players. Steven just looked shocked. When Steven asked why, Brian told him everything would turn out for the best and this had to be done. Brian said he was relieved about the investigation. Brian's father was disappointed, but he understood.

Steven shook his hand and said there was always next year. Steven told him that he wished he was playing with him after all the hard work. Brian told Steven to stay away from The Lucky Leprechaun. Steven nodded okay in agreement. Steven asked Brian if everything was okay, and Brian told Steven with confidence that everything was exactly how he had planned it, and he smiled.

Steven was confused. Brian left before he disclosed too much information. The good news for the team was that Brian and the three other members were allowed to practice with them. Brian was a skilled player and practicing with them would benefit the team.

Mr. Jerome, Mr. Nelson, and Damian arrived three days before the big game. They stayed in the Holiday Inn in Staten Island. They wanted to be as close to Steven as possible. They took a cab from the airport to the hotel. They didn't want to inconvenience anyone. I offered to pick them up, but his Uncle Nelson told us that they were okay.

Steven was so happy to see them. He showed them around the campus. He introduced them to the coach, who was happy to meet them. He mentioned Damian's average football score. Damian had been a college football star. The coach thought it was amazing to have two great athletes in one family. Steven and Damian took a picture with the coach.

Steven stayed in the hotel with them that day. I took the opportunity to have lunch with Kat. Kat asked me how they acted. I told her I only saw them for a short period of time, and they were nice. They loved sports and were very polite. I told her that they were going to do some sightseeing in the city, and I had passed on that too. I wanted Steven to have fun with his family.

I told Kat that I wasn't off the hook that easy. His Uncle Nelson wanted to meet my family. He was more interested when he heard about Aunt Nene. They knew each other. Mr. Nelson even knew my father. He said that the last he heard they were doing well in NYC and that he passed away. They had no information regarding how he passed away. I just smiled.

We made a date so they could meet the family. Steven smiled and said, "Wait until you taste Ms. Amelia's cooking." Mr. Nelson asked me what kind of name Amelia is. I told him it was a Haitian name. He then said that it was a fancy and exotic name. I just smiled.

Mr. Jerome had an awkwardness about him. It was like he wanted to talk, joke around, and get involved, but didn't know quite how to. Mr. Nelson was the smooth one. I acted like I didn't notice Mr. Jerome's weirdness because of Steven. I thought I saw Mr. Jerome staring at me from the side of my eyes, but I ignored it too. I told Kat that he gave me the Rob vibe. Kat gave me her spare bottle of pepper spray and told me not to be afraid to use it. "I don't care who he is, empty the can if he moves wrong and tries to harm you," she said. I told Kat thanks and walked across the hall to my home.

Tracey and the twins were home. I asked them if they felt like seeing Aunt Nene. They were happy and willing to, so I made myself a sandwich and got ready to go. Prince asked about Steven. I told him he was with his uncles and brother and that they were coming over in two days.

Amelia was by Aunt Nene's side when we arrived to King County Hospital, as usual. I told Amelia how Steven's family could not wait until they met and that they were expecting a home cooked meal. Amelia smiled. Aunt

Nene said she would welcome the company, but the best they could get out of her was Kings County cafeteria food.

The visits with Aunt Nene were always nice. I realized how much Steven had become part of the family. I was wondering if Steven missed me as much as I missed him. Prince missed playing basketball with Steven and was looking forward to meeting Damian. Prince had heard so much about him and even spoke to him a couple of times. I was going to see him tomorrow. I knew Prince missed Steven. The visit with Aunt Nene was a good distraction.

I wanted to tell them how weird I felt around Mr. Jerome, but I didn't want to set him up. I just couldn't shake off his weirdness and I wondered how Steven could like him. I gravitated towards Mr. Nelson. He had a personality. He reminded me of Steven.

I imagined that my dad sounded like Mr. Nelson. He had a southern charm, a politeness, a warmness, and a deep voice that commanded attention. I was impressed by his presence. I saw Steven mainly in passing for the next two days. He paged me and we spoke constantly. Steven was telling me how his day was going and how much fun he was having. Steven was getting a kick out of Damian's reaction to the city.

Damian fell in love with New York City. Damian is adventures and flirty so he was ready to plunge in and have fun. Steven was like a kid coming back to tell me everything that happened. I went to sleep happy and was excited about tomorrow.

I was more excited about Steven's family meeting mine than the big game. The next day I woke up early. I helped Amelia season the food that she was going to cook for dinner. Steven had an early practice. It was the last practice before the game. Steven was going to take a cab to his uncle's hotel. Then they were going to take the ferry across to Manhattan. They were going to jump on the "Q" train all the way to Newkirk. Mr.

Nelson wanted to rent a car, but Jerome wanted to see NYC like a true tourist. He felt it wouldn't feel the same if they rented a car. Mr. Nelson had been complaining about public transportation since he got to New York. He missed being able to jump in his car whenever he wanted. I agreed with Mr. Nelson, but I had been waiting for the trains and buses for years. Half the time, if not in a rush, I would just walk to where I had to go.

Amelia was going to cook baked chicken, stewed chicken, black mushroom rice, macaroni and cheese, and fried plantains. She also made a salad. Amelia cooked Haitian dishes, but also made some American dishes just in case they didn't like Haitian food. I made carrot cake and a pineapple upside-down cake. I knew they would love it. I followed my grandmother's recipe. I was baking to impress.

They arrived to the house around 2:30 p.m. Steven led the way. He introduced his uncles and Damian to Amelia. Mr. Nelson smiled at Amelia and told her how gorgeous she was. He said he meant that in the most respectful way. Damian looked at me and then at Amelia and commented on how much we looked alike. Steven just giggled. Jerome complimented Amelia on the house and how good the food smelled. I was shocked that he was participating in the conversation.

Tracey walked in the door from school. She knew that

we were having guests, and she walked in the living room and waved hello. I jumped up to stop her before she ran to hide in her room. I told everyone that she was my baby cousin, Tracey. They must have realized how shy she was. They all introduced themselves one by one.

Jerome stared a little too long. It was uncomfortable for me to watch. Just as I thought he might have been normal, he started acting weird again. They were having a field day talking about their trip to Manhattan. I wished I had time alone with Steven. I just really wanted to hug him. It would be weird for us to just disappear on everyone.

Prince and Princess came home from school. Prince was so happy to see Steven. Steven and Prince did their special handshake that only the two of them knew. Steven looked at Damian and jokingly asked if he was jealous. We all started to laugh. We went around the room to introduce the twins to everyone. Jerome seemed happy to meet the twins. He tried to converse with them as much as he could.

Everyone was talking and then Amelia asked me to set up the table. Steven offered to help me. Tracey started laughing at that, and Damian started to tease Steven. Damian said he would offer to help, but he knew Steven was trying to be alone with Empress. Everyone started to laugh.

We laughed our way to the dining room. I went to grab the Lenox dishes and silverware. Steven started to smile and mentioned that we were going to use the good stuff.

We both started to smile. He gave me a tight hug. He was happy that Amelia was cooking for his family. I went to the living room to tell everyone that we were finished setting up the table.

They looked more than happy to come eat. They enjoyed the food. They loved the stewed chicken, rice, and plantains. Amelia told them that she would pack some for them to go and they were welcome to come eat here until they left. She even asked them what kind of food they liked. Mr. Nelson liked the idea of a home-cooked meal. He looked at Steven and said, "You've got a good one. You are lucky. You came to this big city and found a diamond."

Mr. Nelson turned around and thanked Amelia for being so nice to Steven. Mr. Nelson's voice was trembling, and he sounded like he wanted to cry. He admitted he had been worried about Steven coming to this big city by himself. Steven was finally able to see that his Uncle Nelson loved and cared for him. Steven was holding my hand underneath the table as his uncle thanked Amelia for her generosity. Mr. Nelson cleared his throat, then told us that Damian Sr. came to the city with an old friend and no one ever heard from neither one of them again.

After everyone ate, Mr. Nelson asked about Aunt Nene. Amelia said she was still at Kings County Hospital, but she would welcome visitors. Jerome quickly brought up how one of his college buddies that lived in NYC called him. He was going to meet up with him. Jerome insisted that everyone go visit Aunt Nene without him and he would meet up with them later on at the hotel.

Mr. Nelson was more than okay with that. Mr. Nelson whispered underneath his breath that he was surprised Jerome had friends. I giggled but acted like it was about something else. I agreed with Mr. Nelson that Mr. Jerome is a weird bird. Mr. Jerome left before us, but not before he told the twins if they ever needed anything, they could contact him. Mr. Nelson gave a quiet sigh. I thought it was weird that he showed interest in the twins and acted like Tracey did not exist.

It could be because Prince and Steven were really close and maybe he didn't want to leave out the other twin. Whatever the reason, I felt sad because he excluded my Tracey. Tracey looked unbothered; she probably did not like Mr. Jerome anyway. It took a lot to impress Tracey.

We took two cars to Kings County Hospital to visit Aunt Nene. I rode with Tracey, Damian, and Steven. Amelia drove with Mr. Nelson and the twins. I was asking Damian about Georgia and his football seasons. He was happy to go on about sports. I asked him about Steven's old girlfriends. He started laughing as he said "What old girlfriends. My brother has never liked anyone like he likes you."

I started to laugh and said, "Smart answer." I asked Damian if he ever thought about moving to New York, to which Steven quickly responded that he was not leaving Georgia. He was treated like royalty there. I laughed. I told Damian that I could not wait to visit. I think I would go for the summer.

Steven had a huge smile on his face. Damian was teasing him about wanting to show me off. Damian said that I was even prettier than he had described. He had thought Steven was over- exaggerating. Damian thought Steven had made me up, because no one was that lucky to go to a big city and meet someone special.

Tracey and I smiled. I turned to Tracey and said I had been pretty lucky too, as I was getting into a good family. We all laughed. I told Damian that I couldn't wait until he met my Aunt Nene. Steven laughed and said our relationship had not been official until he met Aunt Nene and Tracey. Tracey giggled. I blew a kiss her way. I embarrassed her when I showed her too much affection in public, but I never cared. Tracey was my baby.

We arrived at the hospital after Amelia. I laughed and asked Amelia to show me her shortcut to the hospital. I kissed Aunt Nene and waited until Tracey greeted her to introduce her to Damian. Aunt Nene took one look at him and told him that he looked like his father while Steven favored his mother. They always got excited to know someone who knew their parents.

Aunt Nene called Steven and Damian the "twin towers." I didn't blame them because I couldn't imagine not knowing any of my parents. They were blessed to have two uncles to look out for them. Mr. Nelson told Aunt Nene it felt good to see someone from the neighborhood that had known his sister and brother-in-law. He looked at Tracey and realized how much they looked alike.

Mr. Nelson told Aunt Nene that Tracey looked just like she had as a kid. He pulled out his wallet and showed everyone the pictures of his wife and children. Damian and Steven were both in that picture. They were shocked that he carried their pictures around in his wallet.

Mr. Nelson especially liked the ones where they had no teeth. He admitted that he used to asked them questions just to hear them talk funny. We all started to laugh. They were a beautiful family. Steven and Damian acted like they were hearing what their uncle was saying for the first time.

We all talked and laugh for hours and then Aunt Nene reminded us of the big game. Steven had to go back to the dorm. His coach wanted him on campus. We all left. I offered to drive them back to Staten Island and would not take no for an answer. Prince offered to come with me. Prince was in heaven being around Steven, Damian, and their uncle. They talked about sports the whole ride. I didn't mind.

I dropped Damian and Mr. Nelson off, then drove to St. John's to drop off Steven. I stopped in front of his dorm building and stepped out of the car to give him a hug. He lifted me up, like usual, and gave me a kiss. Prince and Steven did their secret handshake. I told him that we would all see him tomorrow.

THE BIG DAY

Finally, Steven's big day came. My family was at the gym to support him. We all had St. John's t-shirts and caps on. Kat, Ryan, and R.J. came to support Steven. Slim was even there with Connor and his sisters. Steven had a big crowd that he knew was there to support him. I introduced Mr. Nelson, Damian, and Mr. Jerome to everyone.

Mr. Nelson was equally happy about the game and the friends Steven had made. Mr. Nelson whispered to Amelia that he had no doubt that Steven would succeed in the basketball court, but it was the real world he was worried about. Mr. Jerome just nodded his head in agreement. He sat next to Prince.

Mr. Jerome was asking Prince questions about his school and basketball. Prince answered, but I could tell he was more focused on Steven's game. They were playing Georgetown.

Brian and the other players that were under investigation sat on the bench in full uniforms. They were cheering for their teammates. I could tell that Brian was sad, but he supported Steven. Brian was the closest thing to a best friend for Steven and vice versa. Brian could bullshit everyone but not Steven. Steven appreciated that. Steven was serious, but had a naïve, country personality that demanded respect without asking for it.

Kat sat next to me during the game. We were all laughing and having a good time when all of a sudden, a player from the Georgetown basketball team winked at me. The whole section caught it. I was shocked because I wasn't even into basketball and I only went to Steven's games.

Kat looked at me and said, "There goes Keith starting trouble, of course." I looked closer and it was Keith. Keith knew how we reacted to each other. I had to act like it was nothing because it was just harmless flirting that I had not initiated. I was secretly happy because I knew Keith was meant for great things.

I looked at Kat and told her I was going to get him. Kat smiled and said not if Steven didn't get you first. I looked at Kat and said, "Oops," like a six-year old that made a mistake. Steven must have noticed what Keith did because he just scored on Keith. The crowd was hyped. I was hyped.

I was curious what Keith was up to, but I dared not admit it. It made me wonder if people were meant to follow the same familiar circle. Was I meant to be the girlfriend, maybe wife, of a basketball player? I heard the crowd, which was going crazy over Steven's scoring. I missed the whole thing because I was deep in thoughts. Kat gave me a half side-eye that only a best friend could get away with.

She giggled as if she knew who I was thinking about. I am ashamed to admit that she was absolutely right. For a brief moment, I was in junior high school again.

Steven and the other players were trying hard, but some of the best players were benched and could not play. Steven looked exhausted but determined on that court. Georgetown had an advantage in that all their players were there. Steven would glance up at me like usual during his game. He was like a different person on the court. He looked amazing out there, but he still looked for me.

This is one of the reasons that I made it to every game. Steven always looked for me. When our eyes locked it was like we were the only two there. It's intense. I let him know that I loved him, and I was here for him. I noticed how the family reacted and supported Steven.

We were loud when we had to be and quiet when he was on the foul line. Damian acted like an over-protective brother. He looked like he wanted to run to the court and help him. Prince on the other hand acted like a younger brother. His face was full of pride. I knew he would be talking about this game in school.

Mr. Jerome followed the crowd. He really didn't know much about sports. He just supported Steven in whatever he did. Mr. Nelson could have been a referee or a coach. He missed his calling. Mr. Nelson would get upset at times--not at the team, but the situation.

Mr. Nelson was aware that some of the key players were benched for this game. We all hoped for the best. St. John's and Georgetown were tied for three quarters. St. John's took the lead in the fourth quarter. They were up by 12 points.

Steven's coach pulled him out of the game. I knew it was because he saw how exhausted Steven was. Steven did his best and carried the team this far. His teammates went above and beyond. They were players who hardly played during the season and they were playing toe-to-toe with Georgetown.

This was a monumental moment for them. I am sure their families were proud of them, just as much as we were proud of Steven. This was the first time since the '60s that St. John's was part of the NCAA regional semifinals. The whole city was proud of St. John's University. Georgetown tied with St. John's and there were four minutes left in the fourth quarter. Keith scored a three-point shot. Then Keith teammate was fouled by one of St. John's players. The player made both shots from the free throw line.

St. John's coach got nervous and put Steven and the other four players that he had taken out to rest, back in the game. There was only a minute left in the game. One of Steven teammates must have really been nervous because he fouled Keith. Keith had a smirk on his face as he went to the free throw line. Keith never misses. At least, he never missed since junior high school. Steven and his team played their hardest for the last 30 seconds.

Steven threw a pass to one of his teammates from half court. He caught the ball and scored by the buzzer. They had played well, but in the end, it wasn't enough to win. They did not win the game. His teammates stood up to clap for them. Everyone else stood up and gave them a standing ovation.

St. John's team members, some with tears in their eyes, went and shook hands with the Georgetown team members to show sportsmanship. Georgetown was moving on to compete in March madness. Steven walked to the bench and sat next to Brian.

Brian gave him a playful punch in the arm. I wasn't sure if Steven was acting shy because he lost the game or because of all the attention the team was getting. We clapped, stomped our feet, and sang the school song. We wanted them to know we were proud of them. We celebrated more than the other team. The team went in the locker room.

Our group was waiting for Steven and Brian. We were talking about the game and how well our team played. We all agreed we would do better next year. We were all laughing and talking, and Keith walked over to me and Kat. He smiled like he used to and said he didn't know that I attended St. John's University.

Keith thought I would have attended an out-of-state college. I said I loved the city. I asked him how he liked D.C. He said it was nice, but it wasn't New York City. It was different. I felt someone breathe close to me. I turned around and saw that it was Damian, being a big brother looking out for Steven. He had his arm crossed like LL Cool J would do. Kat and I laughed.

Keith said he didn't want any trouble. I introduced Damian to Keith. I told Keith to meet my boyfriend Steven's older brother, Damian. Keith smiled and said so that's why he dunked on me. I laughed and said probably. Keith admitted that Steven was a good player and if he'd had more support, his team would not have won.

St. John's had them worried and sweating most of the game. Keith asked to meet Steven. He said he was sure he and Steven would meet in the NBA. Keith smiled and said he was a lucky man. Mr. Nelson and Amelia were in the background paying attention to everything. Mr. Nelson smiled and told Amelia that no city slicker was coming in between our family. He laughed and said that we were family now. Amelia laughed in agreement.

Steven and Brian came out of the locker room. I introduced Keith to them. I told them that we went to school together. Steven gave him a firm grip and congratulated Keith. Keith told him that it was good playing with him, and he heard so much about Steven. Steven replied that he had heard a lot about Keith too. They both laughed. Keith told Steven that he should play for Georgetown.

Steven smiled and said he was offered only a sports scholarship there, so he chose St. John's. St. John's had offered him a sport and an academic scholarship. Keith smiled and said, "A double threat!" Keith asked everyone what were their plans for the night? By then, four other Georgetown basketball members joined Keith.

Brian quickly stated that he planned on going to his girlfriend's family bar, The Lucky Leprechaun. Ryan gave the okay nod, as it was safe to go back there. I told him I was in. Kat, Slim, and the Connor sisters were in. We looked at Amelia, Mr. Nelson, and Mr. Jerome.

Mr. Nelson said not to worry about us, "We have old people things to do." Steven was always conscientious. Mr. Jerome laughed for the first time and asked, "Who is old? What are your plans?" Steven reminded Mr. Jerome of The Lucky Leprechaun and informed him what time everyone was meeting up there. Mr. Jerome laughed and said, "I was just pulling your leg.

Go and have fun." I was glad that Jerome wasn't coming. Mr. Jerome's presence would have been awkward for me. He made every situation weird like Mr. Nick. Amelia invited Mr. Nelson and Mr. Jerome to an event my Aunt Dalia was having. She told them that there would be plenty of food and they could meet some more good people.

Steven told them that it would be fun, and he had my Aunt Dalia's food before, and it was amazing. Steven looked at Amelia and said, "It is not better than your food." We all laughed. Keith mentioned that he liked my mom's cooking. Keith was starting trouble and making it sound like more than it was. Keith had Amelia's cooking one time at my graduation party.

Kat put her super best friend cape on and told Keith that she remembered how good the food was at my junior high school graduation party. Kat saved the day again. Amelia told Mr. Nelson and Mr. Jerome that she would meet up with them at the apartment in a few hours. She just had to go visit Aunt Nene. Mr. Nelson told Amelia that he didn't mind visiting Aunt Nene again. Mr. Jerome told Amelia that he remembered he had made plans and couldn't make it tonight.

Mr. Nelson rolled his eyes and whispered, "This is one of the strange things I had to deal with over the years." Amelia just smiled. She told Mr. Jerome, "Next time." I thought it was weird that he had to cancel at the last minute. Mr. Jerome rushed out of there, but not without first saying goodbye to the twins and giving them his contact information. I thought it was weird, but I secretly patronized his behavior in my head for Steven.

Keith left with his teammates, and Chloe, Emma, and Meagan left together. Kat left with Ryan and R.J., and Slim left with Connor. Steven reluctantly left with Brian, Damian, and his teammates. Amelia left with Tracey, the twins, and Mr. Nelson, so I was left to travel by myself. It felt weird because I rarely traveled by myself.

I drove back to Brooklyn thinking how perfect life was for me. I never imagined being in love. Seeing Keith had been a once-in-a-lifetime moment. I hadn't seen him in years. I was happy that he was doing great even though he was acting jealous. I was happy I experienced that heartbreak from Keith because I could more appreciate Steven. I knew he wasn't the same person from that day by the store, but that person helped shape me. Keith was not the same person by the end of that year.

I parked the car on 22nd in Ditmas. I was rushing home to get ready. I wanted to look nice when I met up with everyone at The Lucky Leprechaun. I felt like I was missing out on moments. I was crossing the street on 22nd and Newkirk when a car came out of nowhere.

I remember getting hit and people yelling to call the police and an ambulance. I remember lying on the ground bleeding and not being able to move. I heard three loud noises and I was hoping nothing could get worse. I heard another crowd saying, "Hold him down and don't let him go." I was confused because I was in so much pain and worried about my health.

The ambulance came and the paramedics asked me a lot of questions, which I thought were silly. They put a brace around my neck. I was crying and asking for my mother. The rescue fire workers were trying to calm me down. There was no one that I considered close around.

One of Prince's friends recognized me and said he was going to page Prince for me. I felt relieved among all this craziness. Police officers came and the crowd was yelling, "We got him." I heard one officer ask, "Who shot his tires?" No one answered, but they told the officer, "This is the man that hit the lady at full speed. He didn't stop, it was as if he was aiming for her.

We can't have these things happen on our block."

Tears rolled down my face as I lay wondering who would do this to me. I looked to the side of my face and I saw no other than Mr. Jerome. He had a devilish grin, as if he was satisfied. It felt like a dream. I must have passed out.

SECRETS

My head was spinning, hurting, and my thoughts were racing. I was in so much physical pain. I felt like I'd lost control of everything through no fault of my own. It was like a natural disaster happened, but I was the only victim. I knew I wasn't the only one affected by this, but that's how I felt right then.

I was in the hospital all the time, but it felt different when you're the one hospitalized. The doctors and nurses come in the room at all hours of the day and night. I know it's their job, but every time they came in seemed to be the wrong time. I was glad my friends and family were there when I woke up. There was someone staying with me my whole stay at Kings County Hospital. It was like they took turns.

Steven apologized to me a million times. He was in disbelief, embarrassed, and ashamed. Steven did not want to lose me. He was afraid that I would stop loving him. I acted like I was still asleep when he would cry by my bedside at night. His Uncle Nelson and his older brother Damian visited me to. Mr. Nelson was frustrated and angered about what occurred. He reminded his nephew how he never liked Jerome.

There was something about Mr. Jerome that wasn't right. Mr. Nelson was upset and couldn't understand how a grown man could harm a little girl like me. Mr. Nelson questioned the love Mr. Jerome had for his nephews. No one knew why Mr. Jerome did it.

Steven thought maybe he was jealous of our relationship. Mr. Nelson thought maybe it was because Steven was going to make it to the NBA, and he felt like I was in the way. Maybe he wanted to control Steven more. This man was calculating and cruel. No one saw it coming. Everyone was hurt, saddened, and some were embarrassed.

I was upset because I second guessed myself. I felt something was off with Jerome from the moment I met him. He was just awkward. He would agree to things, find out the details, and bail out depending on who was attending. I liked Steven's Uncle Nelson and his brother Damian from the moment I met them. His Uncle Nelson was a little rough, but I respected that. I respected his honesty and consistency that he showed me in the past two weeks. Aunt Nene liked him too.

Aunt Nene knew his family. She knew Steven's parents very well. She knew more about him then we thought. Aunt Nene didn't want Steven to feel awkward.

Aunt Nene was still in the hospital. They planned on moving both of us so we could be in the same room. The hospital administration was doing this as a favor to Amelia. She is a hard worker and they knew how much she loved her family. What happened to me was a tragedy.

Slim visited me with her future husband and his sisters. She jokingly said I needed to fix my face before her wedding. They were shocked about what happened. Brian was with them. I thought it was sweet of that crazy bunch to visit me. They were loud of course. I had gotten use to that.

They visited me despite going through their own problems. They had lots of rebuilding to do, but they ended up being a cool bunch of people. They made me laugh and joked about how they would get Jerome if he ever got out of jail. I knew they meant it. They were not fooling me.

Slim was caring and relaxed for the first time in years. For a second there, I saw the Slim I met as a kid. She was kind, beautiful, and carefree. She fit right in with that family. She could be herself with them now that she discovered their secrets. She had finally told Connor about what happened to her as a child. He cried. Slim never told anyone about that because she was afraid of being judged or rejected.

Chloe clued us in to what was going on. Chloe looked at me and said, "You are family now, so I can tell you." Four years ago, her father had experienced a stroke. He could not work as much as he used to, and no one really knew the in's and out's of the bar business. Chloe started working there to help out, but she was just a kid to him. Their father didn't want to ask any of his children for a loan because of his pride and health.

Old Nick came to the bar early one day and overheard Mr. Dylan having a conversation with the electric company. Mr. Dylan was embarrassed that Old Nick heard his conversation. He took that moment to offer Mr. Dylan a business proposition.

Old Nick offered to be his silent partner. Mr. Dylan was happy because he already had given up hope and filed for bankruptcy. The Lucky Leprechaun was his life's work. He bought The Lucky Leprechaun after he left the fire department. He raised four children on that income. He was too young to retire and felt too old to start a new job. This was a way to continue doing what he loved.

Old Nick agreed to pay all his debts and gave him

an extra 20 thousand dollars as a sign of good faith. Old Nick told Mr. Dylan that he will be hands off. Old Nick flattered Mr. Dylan with compliments about the bar and the crowd that came there. He wanted Mr. Dylan to host and cater events for him sometimes. Old Nick claimed that he had a better and cheaper supplier for the bar. This was heaven sent for Mr. Dylan.

Everything was great for a few months. Then things started to change. Old Nick was running their business into the ground. He loaned them some money with interest. Mr. Dylan was willing to pay him back, but Old Nick changed the agreement to make it suit him. Old Nick started running numbers in there. He was using the business to launder money and hide stolen goods. He was running illegal numbers.

Mr. Dylan was living in fear for his family. He was losing money. Old Nick would take money as he pleased. Mr. Dylan would have preferred to pay him back but could not. Old Nick was taking money without documenting it. The books were off by thousands of dollars.

Mr. Dylan attempted to speak to him about buying him out, and Old Nick asked about the family. That was an indirect threat to his family. They realized that they didn't know much about Old Nick, and he refused to leave. It would take something extreme to get him to go. Mr. Nick was like a parasite sucking the business dry.

Old Nick wanted to expand his criminal empire when he saw Steven. He wanted to fix basketball games. Old Nick was like a pitbull. Once he got his grip on you, he wouldn't let go. He had big plans for Steven and wanted to ride that gravy train until the NBA. Steven was always with me, so he never got to him, but it wasn't from lack of trying.

Old Nick had approached Brian about tampering with the scoring of the game. He wanted Brian to pull Steven in with him. Brian immediately spoke to Chloe about it. Chloe opened up about their family dilemma. Brian noticed the weird interaction with Mr. Nick and Chloe's family but didn't say anything.

Brian and Chloe were dating for about two months when Old Nick approached him. Brian felt uneasy, but he was madly in love with Chloe. He told Chloe about Old Nick's proposition. Chloe started crying and apologized to Brian. Brian told her it was okay, and he would think of a way to fix it without anyone getting hurt. Chloe tried to talk Brian out of it because she was in love with him. She worried about his safety. She felt like Old Nick would have never met him if it wasn't for her.

Brian spoke to his Godfather, who was also Captain Harris of the 62nd Police Precinct in Brooklyn, NY. Captain Harris called in a favor to have an investigation started. He wanted it to be discreet with little casualty. This was a very sensitive investigation because it involved his family.

Brian had to play along as if he was a money-hungry college kid that didn't know anything. Old Nick asked other teammates who were willing to participate. Brian felt bad for them, but he couldn't trust them with his secrets. Old Nick approached his teammates and they each could have said no.

Brian was hoping they said no, but that didn't happen. He would sometimes try to convince them to stop. Brian approached Steven himself to feel him out. Brian was glad that Steven ignored him and Mr. Nick. He was glad that Steven was a good kid that just loved basketball.

Old Nick was arrested and being tried by the federal government. The feds took the case over due to his money laundering, gambling, drug dealing, tampering with college basketball players, and much more. The NCAA was involved. They penalized Brian and the other players for their own safety. They knew it would have appeared suspicious if there were no consequences for the players.

Slim's future father-in-law, Mr. Dylan, was finally loose from the grip of Mr. Nick. They didn't even mind building the bar back after the fire. They know Old Nick was the person behind the arson, but they couldn't prove it. Old Nick had come by to speak to Mr. Dylan after the fire. Old Nick spoke to him about his ongoing trials and misfortunes.

Mr. Dylan acted like he had empathy for him. Old Nick told him that he could no longer be his silent partner. Mr. Dylan would have to find another way to fund the repair of The Lucky Leprechaun. They were rebuilding the bar after the fire that Old Nick's goons set. He thought he could destroy them, but they didn't care as long as he was out of the picture.

This experience brought the family closer. Old Nick was upset because he was arrested and could no longer control Brian or fix the St. John's basketball games. Old Nick acted like he was saddened about The Lucky Leprechaun being burned to the ground, and Mr. Dylan acted like he believed him. Mr. Nick didn't have any use for the bar or anyone in it.

The bar was hot, the family was happy, and Brian's plan worked. Brian later explained to his parents everything Chloe had told us. Everyone, including Slim and Brian, invested in The Lucky Leprechaun. The Lucky Leprechaun was going to officially be a family business. Brian and Chloe got engaged. Brian wished he could have played in the championship game, but Chloe was more important to him. I fell asleep happy that night because everything had worked out for them.

The next day Aunt Nene was moved into my room. I was very happy. My family would not have to split the visits between us. I was relieved because it meant that Steven and Amelia got a break. I felt really bad for them.

Steven could hardly fit on the couch in the hospital room. I knew his body hurt, but he didn't complain--not even once. Having Aunt Nene as a roommate reminded me of when I used to fall asleep next to Aunt Nene as a child. That was before Tracey was born. I was Aunt Nene's first baby.

I was expecting several visitors today. One of the visits was from Detective Scott. I met him the night of the attack on my life from Jerome. He was in his late 40s and appeared to be in shape. His hair was low cut like the Marines usually wear. Detective Scott was about 5 foot 11 inches tall. He was muscular and had a deep Brooklyn accent. He talked with his hands. He acted like a character from the Godfather, but he had a NYPD badge.

Detective Scott promised that he would bring Jerome to justice. He wanted to update us face-to-face on what was going on. I felt that it was important for my mom, Aunt Nene, Mr. Nelson, Steven and his brother, Damian, to be there. I don't think anyone was ready for what they heard. I knew Steven and Damian were a little hurt and confused by Jerome's actions.

Their Uncle Nelson was in heaven. He had always been suspicious and disliked Jerome with a passion. Mr. Nelson was gloating after the initial shock and anger. He looked at the faces of Steven and Damian; they looked like two six-year-old boys who were told that someone killed Superman. Then he looked at Amelia's face filled with anger because I had been hurt. He understood this was not the time or place to express his sheer happiness of what occurred.

Everyone was in the room talking. Mr. Nelson was discussing old times in Georgia. It was good to see Aunt Nene laughing with someone she knew from her childhood. Everyone was waiting with anticipation to hear what Detective Scott had to say.

Damian pulled out pictures he had developed from their visit to lighten up the mood. This was the first time Mr. Nelson and Damian had been in New Your City. I was sure they would never forget it. Damian must have developed three rolls of film. Everyone was looking at them laughing. Aunt Nene yelled in shock when she looked at one of those pictures.

Everyone asked her what was wrong. With tears in her eyes, she told everyone that Jerome was Kyle's little brother. His name was not Jerome at all. His name was William. Everyone was shocked about his true identity, but my family was even more shocked. Everyone was wondering why William would create a whole fake life.

Kyle was a horrible human being that created so much havoc in our lives.

Aunt Nene explained how William was very intelligent but had been put into a mental hospital when he was 12-years old. William was never right in the head. It was either that or a juvenile detention center.

Kyle would visit him and his family set money aside for him. William killed his cousin, King, because he just did not like him. They found King buried in the woods, one mile away from his house. The town had been looking for William's cousin, King.

William was out playing with him and came back home alone with blood on his clothes. His parents asked him about King, and he stayed silent. He didn't speak to a soul. Everyone including the town sheriff thought something horrific must have happened to William and King. They thought William was in shock.

Everyone was happy he had made it home; despite the fact he gave no details about what happened to King. They found King's dead body three days later. His head was crushed. Forensic officers and the medical coroner's report said King died of suffocation. King was hit in the back of the head with a huge rock and then was strangled. The only bloody fingerprint on the rock was William's. William's bloody fingerprint was also found on King's throat. William was accused and prosecuted for the murder of his cousin King.

William said it was an accident, but all the evidence determined that was a lie. Everyone felt bad for every family member. This kind of behavior was unheard of. William was still a child. Kyle was extremely sad and withdrawn. The only friends he had were my dad and my uncle. The children in the neighborhood would say they were afraid Kyle would kill them.

That is how Kyle really ended up in NYC. Amelia never knew of this. They felt sorry for Kyle. Aunt Nene explained to the others how Kyle was a wolf in sheep's clothing. People trusted him and he betrayed everything and anyone he encountered. Mr. Nelson remembered Williams story. He still didn't have the slightest idea as to why he would try to get close to his nephews.

He hugged his nephews and said, "You two boys are lucky to be here." Aunt Nene told the story of when she first was given hard core drugs. Kyle was responsible for the death of two of her friends. He gave them marijuana laced with crack, PCP, and heroine. Aunt Nene survived but had a long 10 years of addiction. Aunt Nene said living with addiction was a horrible existence.

Amelia hugged Aunt Nene when she told that story. Everyone was waiting for Detective Scott. They wanted to know what new information he had that would make him want to meet with everyone.

Steven was crying as he reminded everyone how William avoided seeing Aunt Nene in the hospital. He made excuses every time. He must have known Aunt Nene would have recognized him. Aunt Nene and William's parents were very close. Their entire family was close. Aunt Nene used to play with William while her brothers played with Kyle.

Detective Scott came in with his partner, Detective O'Neil. He greeted everyone. He said he had good news and bad news concerning Jerome. Aunt Nene asked if he is still in jail. They said he yes. Detective Scott said he was in jail, but that his name was not Jerome. His name was William. We told him that we knew this already thanks to Aunt Nene. She had recognized him from a picture.

Detective Scott told them that William was wanted for murder. There was a cold case from 18 years ago and his fingerprints were all over the murder weapon. It was a cold case that was finally solved. William's juvenile records were sealed so he would have gotten away with it if he hadn't committed this new crime. Everyone was excited about his new murder charges. They felt safe now that he would be in prison for a long time.

Detective Scott said, "I'm sorry to say that there is more bad news." Everyone looked and waited in suspense. Detective Scott disclosed that the murder victim was no other than Steven's father, Damian Sr., Damian Jr., Steven, and Mr. Nelson all started to cry in silence.

Mr. Nelson kept muttering, "How is this possible?" He kept repeating that he didn't understand what was going on. No one understood. Damian said everyone had thought his dad had run away.

Mr. Nelson replied, "Your mother was right when she said that her husband wouldn't just leave his family. Damian Sr. was a young father, but he had a football scholarship. He had his whole life ahead of him. It really didn't make sense that he would run away." Detective Scott informed us that William disclosed Damian Sr.'s identity and why he murdered him.

William planned this because his brother, Kyle, died. William thought Kyle was murdered. He blamed my parents and wanted to hurt them by hurting me. Kyle used to write William and tell him about everything. He told him all his secrets. Kyle must have told William something that made him deeply hate my parents. William confessed to planning this over a decade ago. His main purpose for killing Damian Sr. was to get closer to his children.

Every interaction he had with Steven and Damian was part of his plan to kill me. Every interest he had in their education and sports was to get one of them to New York City. He was trying to get closer to me. I graduated from high school early which worked in William's favor. He was even able to find out the college I attended and talked Steven into accepting St. John's University scholarship offer.

William planned out everything but couldn't plan on the love that Steven had for me. William was what nightmares were made off. William was the reason Steven's mother died. She died of a broken heart when she didn't have too.

Kyle was murdered by drug dealers that he borrowed money from. He still wanted to live the glamorous lifestyle that the twins provided for him. He never graduated from college. Kyle started getting involved in things that he shouldn't have.

One rumor was that they found out he set the twins up after he was arrested on a DUI and turned informant. The worst part is that Kyle stole from my mother, ruined part of Aunt Nene's life, and betrayed friends and family that trusted him. Kyle and William were mean-hearted individuals. Other people's lives did not matter to them.

Detective Scott informed Steven and Damian that their father had a wallet with a picture of his family on him, but they had no idea who he was. He had two gold chains and two rings: a high school ring and an emerald ring.

They always thought Damian Sr.'s murder was personal because he was found with all his jewelry. There was no ID, so whoever had murdered him didn't want his identity found. They didn't want him to have a proper burial. He wanted Mr. Nelson, Steven, and Damian Jr., to fill out some forms to pick up his property. Steven laid his head on my lap and Damian leaned on the wall for support. Aunt Nene walked over to hug Damian.

This news was more of a shock to them. Their whole life could have been different. They could have had their mother and father in their lives. They were loved, even though they had always felt abandoned and unloved. The only person that appeared to give them unconditional love was actually incapable of love. He could mimic love. Their lives were in danger all of their lives and they didn't even know it. The detectives made their way out and thanked everyone for their cooperation. Amelia and Mr. Nelson followed the officers out to thank them.

This had been a hard week for both of our families. Steven lost his championship game; his favorite uncle was a psychopath; and he found out his father had been murdered. I whispered to Steven that I loved him, and I was sorry all these things happened to him. Steven whispered that he was sorry that all these bad things had happened to us.

Mr. Nelson was in a quiet rage. We knew if he spoke a word he would be in tears. He just looked at his two nephews as if they were something amazing. He put his hand on Damian's shoulders and massaged them. He didn't know how to make things better. He finally sat for a second and told the boys how proud he was of them and how much he loved them. He just never thought they cared for him.

Mr. Nelson saw his sister's eyes in their faces. He saw their father's spirits in both of them. Their father was his best friend and the love of his sister's life. They grew up together. Mr. Nelson also felt abandoned by Damian Sr. They had made plans for the future. Mr. Nelson admitted that he was severely depressed when he thought Damian Sr. had just left. He watched his sister die of a broken heart. He saw his nephews get teased and grow up without their biological parents.

Mr. Nelson didn't know how to communicate with them. He didn't want them to see his pain. To children, his behavior made it appear he was being stand-offish. In reality, he was hurt, and he pitied them. He was happy William had helped them in ways he could not, but his protective nature was always cautious. He never was able to figure out William's interest in them.

Mr. Nelson thought William was a pervert and had pulled William to the side to warn him when he first came around his nephews. Mr. Nelson told William that the day he hurt his nephews would be the end of him. Mr. Nelson didn't know he was talking to a psychopath at the time.

I was so happy the twins were not there to hear about their father and uncle. I knew it was hard for my mom to hear about Kyle again. That was one of her mistakes. Steven knew that Amelia was married to Kyle, but he didn't mention it. None of us mentioned it. We were all too busy feeling bad for Steven's family. William ruined a whole family because of his criminal mind. We were all surprised at the length a man could go to for revenge.

Mr. Nelson and Damian had three more days to stay in NYC. Everything had been paid for in advance by William. This trip changed all of our lives. It brought Mr. Nelson and his nephews together. It made me want to go home. I wanted our families to be able to talk, eat, and react freely without concern or feeling as if we were disturbing anyone.

I whispered in Steven's ear to tell him his uncle and brother needed him, so if they wanted to go somewhere with him, he should go. My mom must have overheard and invited Damian and Mr. Nelson to our house.

Amelia promised to cook a gourmet dish for them. Steven smiled and said, "She can really cook, and their house is my second home." Mr. Nelson looked at Aunt Nene and she nodded as if to tell him it was okay and safe. I didn't blame him for being scared. This had been a long day for everyone. I wanted a little space to break down and cry. This was all too much to take in.

I had almost died. I would have never met the love of my life if it weren't for a crazy man. I was sitting up thinking about everything that happened. Who would have thought that a square like William would have been the one that landed me in this condition? He wasn't a square at all. He was a Loogawu, a monster that appeared to be normal, but you could see his true nature only when he attacked.

Some people survive it, but others figured it out too

late. I figured him out, and my face told him too much, and that made him sloppy. Now I was lying in a room in King County Hospital with a broken nose, broken left wrist, arm, and a sprained ankle, surrounded by family and friends. They were all shocked that William did this to me. He appeared quiet and shy, but he too was planning. This was the result of years of built up anger and hatred.

William was just like his brother; a coward, a wimp, a leach that survived off the blood of others. His family caused too much destruction. Kyle got Aunt Nene hooked on crack and also set up my dad and uncle. They both were supposed to die that day. He was in love with Amelia and hated everything about my dad. Amelia discovered that after the twins were born and that was how I ended up where I am. Now, all I could think about was how to live a normal life again.

When everyone left, I went and laid next to Aunt Nene and started to cry. I asked her why this happening to our family. I told her I wished my grandparents were never friends with Kyle's parents. Aunt Nene calmed me down as she held me. She said, "There is good in everything bad if you just look for it.

The universe gives you a special gift every time something bad happens to you. I was given Tracey in my darkest day. Your dad was given your mom and you. You have Steven. Mr. Nelson became closer to his nephews. Your mom had the twins. The universe gives everyone a person to love and hold on too. Steven and Damian were being mentored, even if it was for the wrong reasons. They will have the world in their hands if they can get over this emotional blow."

We were so busy talking that we didn't notice Kat and Slim standing at the doorway. Their visit was unexpected but welcomed. I was shocked to see Kat and Slim together. I hadn't seen just the two of them together since junior high school. They were like oil and water. Slim was an expert in trying to push Kat's buttons. I was glad to see both of them together and not fighting. I really missed us. I missed the way we used to be. They came in asking what was wrong. I told them they would have to sit down for this one.

I started by saying that Jerome was Kyle's brother and his real name was William. William had planned to kill me 17 years ago when I was just a baby. Kat was speechless and shocked. It took a lot to shock Kat. Kat reminded me how I was so nervous about meeting Steven's uncle. I stopped her and told her that that was only the half of it. William was the reason why Steven and Damian were orphans.

William had killed Steven's father in order to get close to them. He had been watching them and entered their lives at just the right moment. William killed his cousin when they were kids and was institutionalized. William was brilliant but insane and lacked any real social skills or empathy for others. He could mimic normal human behavior and emotions, but he wasn't normal.

Slim told me that I was lucky I made it. Aunt Nene told us that she was going to the gift shop at the hospital. She put on her robe, grabbed her bag, and left. Aunt Nene had asked her doctor for permission to go to either the gift shop or the cafeteria. She got bored sometimes and she didn't like to stay in the room all the time.

I loved Aunt Nene, but I knew my friends would not talk freely about things if she was in the room. Kat asked me how Steven and his brother took the bad news. I told her he looked hurt.

Although, I thought his Uncle Nelson took it the hardest. Mr. Nelson lost his sister and his best friend by a man that stayed around his family for years. We never imagined something like that could and would happen to us. The good thing was that William was now in custody for murder and attempted murder.

I couldn't help but think about his wife and children. I wondered if William's wife knew about his true identity. I wondered if she is happy, he's out of her life. Steven had told me that William's kids appeared to be scared of him. I cannot imagine the nightmare that went on in William's house.

I told them how Aunt Nene broke down into tears when she saw William's picture from the basketball game. She was the first to recognize him. This explained why he avoided meeting Aunt Nene in the hospital. Their family was close, and he knew Aunt Nene would have recognized him.

Slim was crying. She was horrified about what happened to me and the depth William took to hurt me. I told Slim it was okay because everything was over now. Kat just rolled her eyes. Kat felt that Slim makes everything about herself. Slim was trying to talk, but her lips were trembling. I patted her back for support.

Slim finally blurted out that she was sorry. I asked

for what. Slim said that years ago she did wish we would get hurt like she did so we would know how it felt. Kat yelled out, "I knew it." I laughed because they were back to normal. One was crying while the other showed no remorse.

I was laughing so hard they both looked at me strangely. I told Slim that William had wanted to hurt me way before she had been hurt, so it wasn't her doings. Slim just laughed as Kat rolled her eyes behind Slim's back. Slim then said she had something else to say.

We both looked at her waiting and secretly hoping she did not say something selfish like she usually did. Slim thanked us for helping her get rid of Rob and Looney. Kat and I looked at each other is shock. Slim said, "I know what you did. I knew for years.

Looney had written me telling how he loved me and took care of Rob for me in a last desperate attempt to be with me. Looney told me how you two rode your bikes up there to tell him about Rob and his work hours. He thought Rob told on him, but I knew how my best friends operated so I know you made sure Looney was caught. I thank you both for this. You could have gotten hurt."

Slim admitted being upset at first because we never told her. I told Slim that she had too much on her plate. She had been physically and emotionally fragile. We didn't want to see her hurt anymore. Slim acknowledged that she understood this now, but she just thought we looked at her different because of what had happened to her.

Slim felt like an outsider and was very angry at us. Kat rolled her eyes and hugged Slim. I smiled at them. I said it was a shame that I had to almost die for things to get back to normal. We all laughed.

I turned to Kat and asked her how she doing? Kat said she was okay. Kat started laughing uncontrollably. We both looked at her wondering what was so funny. Kat said, "Your near-death experience brought me and Ryan closer together." Ryan had been crying and said he could not imagine what he would do if what happened to me were to happen to Kat. Ryan appreciated Kat even more. We were all giving Kat a "high five" and she said there was more.

Tiffany had a job offer from California that paid more and she took it. Tiffany did not think twice about leaving. She promised to keep in touch. R.J. was a little hurt, but he told Kat that Tiffany wasn't as much fun as she was. Ms. Dorothy winked at me when Tiffany was saying goodbye. Ms. Dorothy knew Tiffany wasn't going to stay. Ms. Dorothy was glad to see Tiffany leave. Kat was glad to see Tiffany leave too.

We were catching up on everything when Nurse Amy walked in saying she had good news. She asked for Aunt Nene. I told her she had gone to the gift shop. Nurse Amy told me that we would be discharged today. I smiled because I was ready to be at home with the rest of my family. I was ready to be there for Steven. I wanted to be there for my mom, Tracey, and the twins. I wanted to be in my own room.

Aunt Nene walked in few minutes later. I told her that Nurse Amy said we were being discharged. Aunt Nene was happy. Kat offered to take us home since we lived in the same building, and we took her up on her offer.

I decided to call Amelia just in case they thought about coming back to the hospital.

The ride home was different than any ride I ever had in my life. I looked at every street and all the people walking through different eyes. Certain parts of the city felt foreign to me. I had to do a double take in order to recognize places I had seen hundreds of times. The whole week felt unreal. I felt like I was watching someone else's life.

I understood how Slim felt. I was scared, even though I had support and had been helped immediately. Slim must have felt a hundred times worse. She was attacked several times. The person who was supposed to protect her had turned her back on her. She left her home with nowhere to go.

Slim had been very young and didn't have a positive support system until she came back to us. She could not take it anymore. We were her help, yet we were younger and more naïve than she was. I always saw Slim's pain, but now I felt it. People truly do not understand things until it happens to them.

I felt a weight lifted off my shoulders when I got to the building. I was relieved, but I knew Slim hated her old home with good reason. Slim usually made excuses not to come in. This time, I tried to make an excuse for her. Slim kissed me on my forehead and said, "It's okay. I will come in this time."

We arrived at the house to my family and new friends laughing and eating. Tracey and the twins ran up to Aunt Nene and I to hug us. Tracey was acting delicate with me and gave me a look of pity. I smiled and told her everything was okay now and would be alright. She smiled.

Steven was standing in the corner smiling. He was letting the kids ask me questions so he could greet me last and have me more to himself. I looked back at him and had a smirk on my face. Kat noticed it and started laughing, then said, "There go those two love birds." Damian noticed it too and just shook his head and smiled. I realized at that moment; I had found the love I always wanted.

Steven loved me during the worst and best of times. He was a man that would protect me and love me in good times and bad. I had the love that was destined to be. He was my twin soul. We were born in different parts of the country but found our way to each other in the most unusual way.

Amelia cooked a big dinner. Kat and Slim stayed. I was happy Aunt Nene and Tracey were going to stay. They always stayed for about a week or until Aunt Nene was ready to leave.

Mr. Nelson, Damian, and Steven took a cab to the Holiday Inn on Staten Island. Steven looked like he didn't want to leave. I told him it was okay because his brother and uncle needed him. I could see they were hurting, even though they were laughing, eating, and talking about sports and their families. They showed interest in the Haitian culture. They loved the food and were fascinated by the Haitian history.

I kissed Steven goodbye. Kat and Slim stayed for about 30 more minutes. Slim decided to spend the night at Kat's house because it was getting late. Slim called her grandparents and Connor so they wouldn't worry about her. I thanked them for staying and coming to see me. Kat just rolled her eyes and asked, "Are you serious?" We all started to laugh. They left and promised to come back. I rolled my eyes at them and started to laugh because now they were being sensitive.

Amelia called everyone into the living room for a family meeting. Amelia looked like she was going to burst into tears. Aunt Nene sat next to her and was rubbing her back. Amelia apologized for everything that happened even though it wasn't her fault. She apologized for not being able to protect us like she should have. I told Amelia that it was okay. She said from today on, there would be no more secrets.

Amelia started to cry. She said she realized only the truth could keep us safe. She had thought by keeping things hidden, we would be safer. Amelia explained that she was young when certain decisions were made that were now affecting us and other people. Amelia said she wasn't perfect, and her decisions were based on love and she wasn't thinking about the future. She didn't think her decisions would lead to anyone getting hurt. Amelia told us she did her best with us and she never meant to hurt anyone.

She was just in love and wanted a happy life. It cost her and other people a lot. Amelia explained she didn't regret her decisions, because her children would have never been born. She just wished she would have moved away with our father instead of waiting for the right time. Time always won.

I told Amelia it was okay, and no one knew that

William and Kyle were crazy. The twins put their heads down because that was their father and uncle. Prince said, "I hope I don't turn out that crazy." Amelia said it was okay and that he wasn't anything like them. Aunt Nene looked at Amelia and said, "It is time." Amelia said she knew.

We all sat there in silence wondering what they were talking about. Amelia started by telling us how she met Kenneth and how much in love she was with him. She met his twin brother, Lenny, too. They were very nice, quiet, and country. They were new to the city and so was she.

Kenneth, for some strange reason, understood the Haitian culture. He was not pushy. He was humble and not flashy. He was like no other man she had ever met in her life. He later confessed to her what he did for a living. He said his reputation surpassed the truth. He was lucky enough to never have to use a gun despite what he did. He had been arrested one time.

Kenneth and Lenny were ready to stop everything. They had had enough and wanted to leave New York City for good. Kenneth and Lenny were in the business of transporting and supplying drugs to drug dealers. That didn't make it better. Their work was eating their souls whenever they passed someone who was an addict. They heard about the crack babies and it made them cringe. It was no longer a job without a face or victim. Innocent victims were getting hurt. Everyone knew they were going to quit and move. However, they quit too late.

One day Kenneth and Lenny went out to collect money from a person they supplied a large amount of drugs too. That was their last collection. They had two armed bodyguards. They did not even carry weapons. They were the only persons that Chinaman trusted with the money. It was a sting. They and their client were set up. The client thought it was them and started shooting.

Their security guard was shooting, and the FBI was shooting. That was the day the world thought Kenny died and Lenny was locked up. Later, we found out that they had an informant. Amelia and Aunt Nene were crying while Amelia was telling the story. I held on to the twins and Tracey and said we knew the story. I even mentioned that I knew who Chinaman was. Amelia shook her head.

Amelia said it was over at the trial. They discovered that the informant was Kyle. He was showing off one night at a bar bragging about the twins and how he could get his hands on anything, and people needed to respect him. He bought drinks for everyone at the bar, laughing and having a good time.

Kyle didn't know there was an agent sitting two seats away from him, drinking the beer Kyle had bought and taking mental notes of everything he was saying. Kyle left the bar extremely drunk. The agent stopped his car a few blocks away from the bar. They interrogated him. Kyle told them everything he knew about the twins. He even brought the agent around them.

Kyle had a habit of bragging about the twins and threw their names around frequently. People gave him free things and he met a lot of women that way. Kyle was just an attention-seeking leech. I felt bad for the twins listening to this. Amelia must have followed my eyes looking at the twins and noticed how sad they looked. They never met Kyle; they just knew he was their father.

Amelia looked at them and me and said, "This is the hardest secret I had to hold in my life. I only told it to your Aunt Nene." We all looked at her waiting in anticipation. She looked at the twins and told them that Kyle was not their father. Their father was also Kenneth. Kenneth knew that his job was dangerous, so he participated in sperm cryopreservation just in case he died. His sperm was frozen before I was born.

Lenny did the same thing, but never met his special someone. Amelia used Kenneth's sperm when she married Kyle. This was the perfect time to have children and no one would ask questions. Kyle never knew about this. That was probably why the twins were never a target for William. He thought they were his nephew and niece.

William show interest in them for the brief moment he was around them. We all were shocked, except for Aunt Nene. The twins were relieved that Kyle wasn't their father. It was hard to know that they came from a family with so much mental and criminal flaws. They were relieved that Kenny was their father. They were sad because they never met him. I told them it was okay because she wasn't finished. Amelia explained why she had to marry Kyle.

Very few people were able to tell the difference between Kenny and Lenny in New York City. While Kyle was testifying, he realized that it was Lenny that died, not Kenny. Amelia knew all along that Kenny was still alive. She didn't say anything because Kenny would have been charged with King Ping status and never come out of prison.

The FBI and police officials could not tell the difference. They were identical twins, so they shared the same DNA. Lenny died in Kenny's arms. They protected each other and were hardly ever apart. When they called Kenny by his brother's name, he just stared. He was in shock at first, but then he realized this was fate smiling at him just a little. He felt horrible for living and even worse when he couldn't protect his family from Kyle. He couldn't protect Amelia or Lenny.

Kenny was in shock when he saw it was Kyle testifying against him. Kyle had approached Amelia later. Kyle told Amelia that he knew that was Kenny and would tell the FBI that they are prosecuting the wrong brother if she didn't marry him. Amelia married him, reluctantly.

Amelia visited Kenny and, with tears in her eyes, told him that Kyle had this crazy idea that he was alive, and he wanted to marry her. He would expose this if she didn't marry him. Kenny sat there in silence. He was sorry that he brought this psycho, Kyle, into her life. This is when he figured out that Kyle had always been jealous of him.

Kyle wanted everything he had. Kyle was a horrible friend that ruined his escape out of the drug game and got his brother killed. He separated him from his family, and now he wanted his family. Kenny didn't speak at all the whole visit. He just sat there in silence while tears ran down his face.

Tracey turned around and asked Aunt Nene, "You knew all this?" Aunt Nene said she was told about this about 12 years ago. Amelia opened up to her when she didn't know what to do about her addiction. Aunt Nene had hit rock bottom of her addiction and didn't want to live. Aunt Nene was ashamed and embarrassed and didn't know what to do. She also never shared what Kyle did to her.

Amelia had a heart-to-heart talk with her and explained how she was responsible for her. She promised her brother that she would look after her. Amelia was taking all the blame and said she could never face Kenny again. That is when Aunt Nene said, "Tell who what?" Amelia tried to change the subject, but Aunt Nene would not let it go. She told Amelia you have to tell me the truth.

Aunt Nene explained what Kyle did to her and her friends. This had happened before the trial. No one knew how much of a snake Kyle was. Amelia told Aunt Nene the truth and told her this was a dangerous secret. Aunt Nene was always getting high, so she never cared about visiting her brother Lenny. This information was like a miracle to her. She didn't favor one brother over another, but a miracle is a miracle.

Aunt Nene and Amelia had gone to visit Kenny. Kenny was in shock. He was happy but sad to see his baby sister strung out on drugs. Aunt Nene winked at Kenny like they used to wink when the twins would play tricks on adults. Kenny understood that she would not say a word and keep the family secret.

Kenny spoke to Aunt Nene like he did when she was a child. He spoke to her with love. Aunt Nene started to cry and told Kenny what Kyle did to her. Everyone was crying. Aunt Nene never used drugs again.

She volunteered years later at the prison he was housed at. Aunt Nene needed a reminder of who she used to be.

Amelia looked at all of us and said, "This is how one man caused so much hurt to a family. The worst part was that Kyle didn't want to go away.

Kyle thought that he would be protected if he married me. No one would suspect what he did to the twins and everyone that was arrested and died in that FBI sting. Kyle made himself more important than he really was. People did not know him and the ones who knew him took him as a joke. They humored him because of the twins. Everyone who really knew him did not associate with him once Lenny and Kenny were gone.

Kyle could have continued to go to school or disappeared. Instead he had the audacity to make himself a fixture in Amelia life. Kyle tried using Amelia name to open doors for him, but anyone who knew Chinaman knew dealing with anyone who mentioned his children was a no. This is what I hid, this I did for the love of family. This is the secret William knows. This is why he hated us. He thought we retaliated against his wretched brother Kyle.

Kyle died because of his own greed and negative actions. He messed with the wrong people and didn't have anyone to protect him. Kyle was the reason for his own death." Kenneth had not put Amelia and his children in harm's way by exposing Kyle. Kenneth knew about the twins. Amelia sent him pictures of them. Amelia looked at us and said, "I want everyone in this room to always be aware of who is around you." I was glad she told us everything. I was even happier that Kyle was not the twin's father. I never knew what Amelia saw in him; I had never liked Kyle anyway. I knew this was a secret that I dare not ever share.

Printed in the United States
By Bookmasters